THE WIZARD OF BOLAND

Because he doesn't have a supply of dragon's blood, wicked Wizard Homm finds it difficult to try some of the better spells given in his book *Wizard Wizardry*. One day he gets lost in the mysterious Forest of Boland and what should he see there but a dragon! He manages to get a a small bottle full of its blood—which is a bright turquoise blue—and then he is able to work all sorts of new spells. But many of them are bad spells, and so when Helda the goose-girl, who is also lost in the forest, meets the Wizard, she is in real danger.

A sequel to *The Forest of Boland Light Railway*, available in Knight Books.

'BB'

The Wizard of Boland

Illustrated by D. J. Watkins-Pitchford

KNIGHT BOOKS

Hodder & Stoughton

ISBN 0 340 04183 8

Copyright © 1959 Edmund Ward (Publishers) Ltd
First published 1959 by Edmund Ward (Publishers) Ltd

This edition first published 1970
Third impression 1977

Printed and bound in Great Britain in Knight books for Hodder &
Stoughton Children's Books, a division of Hodder & Stoughton Ltd,
Arlen House, Salisbury Road, Leicester by
Richard Clay (The Chaucer Press) Ltd, Bungay, Suffolk

Contents

1

THE WIZARD IN HIS CAVE

WIZARD HOMM sat at the entrance to his cave enjoying the warm spring sun. This cave was among the ferny rocks on the verge of a vast wild forest which was called the Forest of Boland. It was sheltered from the north winds by the sturdy oaks and other forest trees and from where the Wizard sat he could look across the valley, away to the misty blue rim of the downs. On a crystal-clear day he could sometimes even glimpse the bright sword-blade gleam of the open sea.

Below him, across the brown stream, which was called the Boland Water, beyond the ford and its wooden bridge, was the village. It wasn't much of a place to look at, not by our present-day standards. The houses were mere wooden huts thatched with straw; from a distance they looked like bee butts set in a row, and the people moving in and out resembled bees, crawling on their alighting boards. There was quite a high wooden palisade around the village in which was a tall wooden gate. This was always closed at night, for the houses were too close to the Forest to be comfortable.

Beyond lay the cultivated grounds, strips of tilled

golden-red earth, rather like allotments, where the villagers grew their crops. Some of the better-off peasants kept cattle, big, white, slow-moving oxen which they used for ploughing, as well as for milking, and of course geese, lots and lots of white cackling geese. Every evening they had to be driven in from the shallow ford where they so often spent the day.

Wizard Homm did rather well out of the ignorant peasants. They paid him good money for special spells, spells to make the harvest a good one, spells to bring rain or to stop it coming, spells to bring a boy baby instead of a girl (and the other way round). The Wizard was a long, thin man. It would be hard to say how old he was because Wizards, like ladies, never let on how old they are. He hadn't a pleasant face even though he wore a long white beard. His nose was too thin and snipey, and his eyes were set rather too close together; his mouth was mean and thin-lipped, and his teeth were badly in need of a dentist. I must say his eyes were rather frightening, for they were very dark, very small, and they glittered like black diamonds.

He wore a sort of voluminous nightgown, dark blue in colour, sprinkled all over with a pattern of silver stars. This material he had picked up cheap at a local jumble sale. Actually it had once been curtains which hung in Boland Castle – which was about a mile from the village round the next bend of the stream – but the villagers didn't know this.

On his head he wore a black hat shaped like a

chimney-pot. It had no brim. It was exactly like those worn by Greek monks today. I don't know where he got it from, but it impressed the peasants.

I'm afraid he wasn't a very clean old man; in fact, the last time he had a bath was when he accidentally fell into the Boland Water two years before, as he was catching frogs with which to make spells.

His only companions were three kittens, Ding, Dong, and Belle. He had reared them himself on goat's milk. They were orphaned cats. Their mother had been stewed in the Wizard's pot to make a specially potent spell (he was always experimenting), but of course the kittens didn't know this, because they were blind and helpless when the Wizard took charge of them.

He could speak to them in their own language, so you see he really was a Wizard, even though his spells were unreliable.

Now he sat at the door of his cave stirring some evil-looking mixture in a large black pot over a fire. That morning he had received a visit from one of the peasants in the village who had paid him quite a lot of money for a special spell to make the corn grow.

From where the Wizard sat he could see this same peasant, whose name was Halberd, busy sowing his corn on the tilled ground beyond the village. Halberd was sowing the grain by hand. He had a flattish wicker basket of rather a beautiful shape slung in front of his chest. As he strode rhythmically along he dipped first one hand into the basket and then the other, throwing the seed to left and right in a fan-like spray. A little cloud of orange-coloured dust hung behind his cross-gartered legs as he strode to and fro, for there had been no rain since the middle of February, and the earth was powdery.

Not far off was Halberd's house, where he lived with his wife and his rather naughty, but very pretty little daughter, Helda. Helda was a goose-girl. She looked after her father's geese, taking them out in the morning to the water meadows by the stream and herding them back at night. It was rather a jolly life, and in summer all her waking hours were spent in the open air.

In the long winter evenings she did lessons – that is to say a kindly old hermit called Dombrass, who had a wart on his nose (he was tutor to the Lord of the Manor's sons) gave her reading lessons – in Latin, of course. In return, Helda's father gave the hermit eggs, cheese, and skimmed milk, and lambs' tails in the spring for pies.

Helda liked the summer better than the winter because she didn't have to work at her Latin. One day she was to find these lessons very useful, as we shall see.

She wore no shoes or stockings, and she was as hard and as brown as a gipsy. She had raven-black hair, black brows, large eyes of a wonderful blue-green colour, fringed with long soft lashes, and a nose that was turned up cheekily at the end. Like the Wizard and the rest of the people in the village, she never had a bath.

As Halberd strode to and fro across his dusty field he could see the Wizard sitting at the door of his cave under the edge of the trees. He hoped that he was inventing a good spell, a spell which would not only make the corn grow straight, thick, and tall but also one which would keep the wild boars and deer from damaging the crop, for his cottage was very near the Forest.

But to tell you the truth, Wizard Homm, even though he had charged poor Halberd two pieces of silver, was making a spell of quite another kind.

A few days before, when he had gone down into the village to do his weekly shopping, naughty, pretty Helda had acted in a very rude way. As soon as she saw him coming she had danced before him down the street singing:

> 'Him Homm Humbledon
> Ding Dong Bell!
> Four foul fishes
> For our deep dark well!'

Then she had run into the hut and slammed the door, which I think you will agree was very rude indeed. And all the geese came chattering and hissing at his heels.

Wizard Homm was not at all amused. He said nothing to her father, but took his money just the same, and determined to get even with Helda, which just shows what a nasty, sneaky, old Wizard he was. He would have dearly liked to turn her into a rabbit or a frog, but that (at the moment at least) was beyond his powers. So he 'wished her away', wished her away into the Forest, and once anyone went into the Forest that was the last you saw of *them*. What a thing to do on such a lovely morning!

So Wizard Homm stirred and stirred his big black pot which gave off a most appalling smell of I don't know what, and he wished her away into the Forest of Boland and hoped the bears would gobble her up.

Meanwhile, poor Halberd, swinging up and down the dusty field, felt a glow of contentment. This crop would be a fine one, now he'd paid Wizard Homm for a really good spell, and the lovely spring sun seemed to make the world a very delightful place, which indeed it was on that glowing April morning.

2

A SURPRISE FOR THE GNOMES

WIZARD HOMM, even though he was a Wizard never ventured far into the great Forest behind his cave. Nor did the peasants from the village. Of course, there was no danger in going into the *fringes* for firewood, and, indeed, in autumn some of the peasants turned their hogs into the outskirts to eat the acorns. Pigs, both tame and wild, love acorns. To each pig was attached a bell, and a heavy piece of wood was slung crosswise from their necks to prevent them from straying. Always there was a pig boy with them.

Humans were well advised to keep out. For mile after mile the great oaks grew, and dense bramble brakes and green shielding fern made impenetrable thickets. There were no paths or tracks save those made by animals, the wild boars, deer, wolves, and the lesser four-legged people of the wild.

In addition to animals which we know already, either from pictures, or zoos – animals such as wild boars, deer, badgers, foxes, wolves, and bears – there were a host of creatures which no human had ever seen, not even Wizard Homm. There were cowzies, strange furry rabbit-sized little animals, armless, but clothed in fur. They looked like animated pin-cushions. They roamed the Forest in packs of from fifteen to fifty, their teeth were sharp, their sense of smell and eyesight keen. There were cotton-rod rabbits, and henheads, partridge-like birds, very stupid, and extremely good to eat; there were stopplepeckers – birds of the woodpecker tribe, the size of crows, with powerful beaks, and barred with black and white and touched with brilliant scarlet on the head, wings, and flanks.

At one time there had been leprechauns, but these had now been banished.

By far the most important people of the Forest were the gnomes, of whom there was a colony of one hundred and three, counting the lady gnomes which were called 'wombies' and the children which were called 'gombies'.

Their Chief was named Hal o' the Hobb. He had many sons and many wives. His eldest son was called Lobgob. Lobgob was the cleverest of them all. He had made a railway called the *Forest of Boland Light Railway* and had built a lovely little engine called the Boland Belle. I have already told the story of this railway in another book. The making of the engine and the railway and all the perils and adventures undergone in its construction are old history now.

The main purpose of this railway was to serve the mines where the gnomes dug for gold and other metals. Every day miners set out for the day's work. They lived, you see, some way from the mines, at a place called Boland Banks. There, above the dark Boland Water, they had lived for years beyond counting, deep and secure as badgers in their little houses under the twisted grey roots of the tall beeches.

Their houses were the cosiest imaginable. Holes bored through the grey smooth cable-like roots acted as windows, and for glass they used horn. They slept in little beds, just as we do; they had fireplaces, ovens, tables, chairs, and rugs and carpets made of skin and woven fibre. They had no television or wireless because Lobgob hadn't got around to that yet. Probably the gnomes were a lot better off without such luxuries and time-wasters. In any case, there was so much work to do all day long and every day that they had little leisure.

Unlike most of the peasant children outside the Forest, the gombies had to go to school. They learnt how to do sums, and the history of their own tribe and its past deeds, but their chief lessons were to do with the life of the Forest, the habits of the wild

animals and birds, the names of wild flowers and herbs. The boy gombies had to spend many hours a week at shooting practice with bows and cross-bows; they were taught how to make springes, deadfalls, and snares, and most important of all, the arts of fishing and tracking. The girl gombies learnt cookery (most necessary this, because all gnomes are fond of food), how to make wines from berries and herbs, a certain amount of first aid and 'gombie craft' – that's baby craft – and, of course, every girl gombie had to learn to sew, knit, and weave.

Unlike humans, who do not live very long, the gnomes lived for hundreds of years. Because of this they didn't have so many children as we humans do, which was a very wise provision of nature. I don't suppose there were more than a couple of gombies born each year, so there was no danger of the population growing unmanageable.

Now I have given you a brief picture of the inhabitants of this great Forest of Boland. Let us see what they are up to on this bright morning of spring on which my story begins.

Just as in our own world grown-ups, and children too, have work and lessons to do, however bright the world outdoors, so the gnomes could not spend all their time enjoying themselves. The gombies had to be at their lessons in the school at Boland Banks (under the watchful eye of their schoolmaster whose name was Pokenose), and most of the strong able-bodied gnomes were hard at it in the depths of the new mine at Poolewe. This mine contained plenty of gold; it was by far the richest mine in the whole Forest. It had been discovered only a year or so before, quite by accident, and a branch line had been constructed so that the miners were saved all the labour of walking there from their homes at Boland Banks. In the past this mine had been the scene of great happenings.

Leprechauns, led by Shera Beg, had, by a most dastardly trick, once captured the entire gnome colony at that historic spot.

Now, with the leprechauns well out of the way, and banished from the Forest, work had gone on apace. The gnomes had driven their galleries farther and farther into the solid rock. Much rich treasure they had found; the farther they burrowed into the hill, the richer the veins of gold. From this precious, most beautiful, shining metal they fashioned wonderful goblets and bowls, most exquisitely chased and wrought, and some of it they melted down into money.

So now, on this fine morning, let us leave the sunlight and the green Forest, the song of the birds, and the sweet scents of fern and bank and enter the dark shadowed mine at Poolewe.

The long mysterious corridor was lit by small lanterns suspended from the roof. It smelt dank after the sweet fresh air of the Forest outside, and as the railway line wound its way farther into the shadows the sound of picks and shovels could be heard, echoing strangely in the confined space.

About two hundred yards inside the hill the

gnomes were busy at the rock face. They heaped their little barrows with stone and earth. When they were full they were emptied into the waiting trucks. A signal was given and their fine engine, the Boland Belle (which all this time had been waiting quietly simmering, the glow from the fire-box shining on the mine roof) would start with a great banging of buffers and gouts of steam and away it would go, out into the sunlight where another gang of gnomes was waiting down by the bridge to wash the rocks and earth, 'panning' as it is called with us.

Lobgob, the gnome who built the engine, was inside the mine, stripped to the waist, wielding a heavy pick. Gurtweed, Snurt, Sneezerod (who had once been the ticket clerk and had delivered the entire gnome colony from the power of Shera Beg), yes, he was there too, working with the rest.

Clink! clank! went Lobgob's pick as he drove it into the rock. Trickles of earth came down, and dust got into his large nose and made him sneeze.

I suppose that Lobgob was no more than eleven inches in height. As a matter of fact, the gnomes varied in height from ten inches (average) to twelve inches, which was tall for a gnome. The wombies were rather shorter, about nine to ten inches, but more broad in the beam. All were immensely strong. You see – a mole, for its size, is very strong, compared with ourselves, and for that matter, so are ants. Were we half as strong as ants, in proportion to our size, we should be able to lift enormous weights. It was the same with the gnomes.

So it's not surprising that they could make such headway in the hard rock of the mine; but it was not easy work, for all that, especially on a beautiful sunny day!

I must say that Lobgob found the toil rather irksome. He couldn't help thinking of the sunny Forest, of how bright the stream would be, sparkling at Boland Water, how the fish would be biting. Gurtweed, his brother, working the seam close by, was wishing he was away in the glades with his new wombie, for he had been married only a week. Lobgob, being as yet unmarried, did not worry so much on that score, but he would have liked to go fishing.

However, it was no good thinking of other things; any moment now the Boland Belle would be coming back with a train of empty trucks, and Lobgob had to fill his barrow before it returned.

Clank! clink! went his pick, more dust came into his eyes. At last his barrow was full. He sat down on a rock and waited. Three more barrow-loads must be filled before it was time for lunch in the canteen outside the mine, where a crowd of wombies were busy around a big black pot, from which issued delicious smells of cooking.

At last there came the echoing rumble which grew louder every moment. The Boland Belle, pushing her three trucks backwards, came pounding down the line. The driver that morning was Grout. Grout had only just learnt to drive the engine and he was very proud of the fact. Usually it was Lobgob's task, though the gnomes liked to take it in turns, as was only right; for after all, driving an engine is great fun.

Soon Lobgob could see the dirt-stained trucks backing and wriggling slowly down the dimly lit line. The nearest one drew up with a great banging of buffers close to the rock face. Lobgob emptied his barrow. Then, back he went again to the rock face, and whack! whack! went his pick.

He was hard at it and his barrow was half full when a most curious and rather alarming happening took place.

He had driven his pick well into the stone where there was a sudden ominous rumbling and he was enveloped in a cloud of dust which was so thick it dimmed the feeble light of the lantern hanging from the roof. The pick in his hand, which he had driven with some force, seemed to cartwheel away from him, and vanish into the darkness in front!

Lobgob's first thought was that the roof was coming down; actually, it was nothing of the sort. He had apparently broken into the entrance of a natural passage in the rocks. Instead of a solid wall in front of him there was now a gaping cranny, a couple of feet wide, as black as ink!

Not only that but as this crack opened, a rush of air fairly whistled down the passage and blew out the roof lantern.

Luckily, just at that same moment, Grout had opened the door of the fire-box under the boiler to put on more wood, so there was still enough light for Lobgob to scramble for shelter under the nearest

truck. He dived under-
neath it and lay there, between the metals, pant-
ing. He quite thought
that the roof was coming
down. From time to time
they had roof falls in the
mines, even though pit
props were used for sup-
port.

a stopplepecker

It took some moments
for the dust to settle, and
for the echoing rumble to
die away. Other gnomes,
from nearby workings,
came hurrying to the
scene with lanterns, looking anxiously about
them. Lobgob crawled
out from under the truck in rather a shame-faced
manner, and with the rest of the miners he made an
examination of the large crack.

It was pitch black beyond, as I have said, but this
did not deter Lobgob, who snatched a lantern from
the nearest hand and climbed boldly over the rubble.

He found himself in a great cleft in the rock about
two feet wide but with no visible ceiling. The crack
seemed to soar away into upper darkness which even
the light of the lantern failed to illuminate; it was
as high as the roof of a cathedral nave.

Underfoot was hard smooth rock, and as Lobgob,

23

followed closely by over a dozen miners, went farther in, the walls of the crack became wider and wider until at last, after walking about thirty yards, they found themselves in an enormous cavern. If you have ever been to the Cheddar Gorge caves in Somerset you will have some idea of the wonderful sight that met their eyes.

Huge stalactites and stalagmites decorated the walls and ceiling and the flickering feeble light of the lantern, shining upon these, cast weird and wavering shadows like huge tilting spears. On every hand was seen the glint of specks of gold which was almost dazzling. But the most thrilling sight of all was a band of what appeared to be solid gold which ran diagonally across one wall like a belt. Hardly believing their eyes, the gnomes drew closer, and Lobgob, holding the lantern close, saw that it was indeed *solid gold*, a band of it quite a foot wide and many more in length.

Hitherto all the gold they had found had been hard to quarry; most of it was in small particles hidden in the loose shale of rock and sand. But here was enough, more than enough, to make a million, million drinking goblets, bowls, and bracelets – why! they could build a house of gold with the amount they saw before them!

They were all so busy with this immense and fabulous treasure that they did not notice a rather curious sound which was coming from the far end of the cave, which was, of course, in utter darkness. I can only compare it to the slow deep murmur of the sea, the sound made by great waves as they advance and recede upon a steep and pebbly beach on a calm day, *a huge, quiet, breathing sound*!

It was Lobgob who noticed it first. He hushed the babel of tongues about him and stood facing the darkness in front.

They were quite at a loss as to what the sound could be, and, to tell you the truth, all felt a little scared. It was like no sound they had ever heard before.

Lobgob, ashamed perhaps of his earlier behaviour in creeping under the truck, determined to go forward and investigate. Cautiously he followed the slightly sloping floor of the cave towards the farther end, if indeed the cave did end at all. And as he moved the sound became louder. He was aware, too, of a strange odour which resembled the smell of weeds on a weir, a sort of wild, wet, river smell, half rotten, but nevertheless not at all unpleasing.

Peering forward, Lobgob at last caught a glimpse of something gleaming wetly in the rays of the lantern (which he held aloft with a trembling hand).

As he drew ever nearer, one cautious step at a time, this gleaming, winking light was seen to be the reflection from what appeared to be *the end of a scaly tail*, but a tail so vast that it passed imagination!

Closer went Lobgob until he was within a foot of it. The body to which it belonged was lost in the darkness beyond, from which the sound of breathing came, a sound which was now very loud indeed – as if the creature, whatever it was, were fast asleep. Lobgob and the following gnomes were thunderstruck with astonishment. They had forgotten all about the gold, way behind them.

Lobgob, not without acute fear, held the lantern closer still to the tip of the tail which was, at the very end, tapered to a blunt point and about as thick as a human boy's body. (Of course, to the gnomes, who were very small, this seemed colossal.) It looked like the tail of a gigantic worm.

Yes, there, plain to see, were the hard scales, each overlapping the other like armour, beautifully fashioned, and becoming smaller at the very apex, each gleaming with wonderful iridescent colours, greens, bronzes, and blues, shading to a sort of silvery white on the underside.

Growing very bold now (for the creature still seemed fast asleep and quite unaware of their presence), the gnomes pressed forward and noted, with every step, how the tail bulked higher until, when they reached the part where it joined the body, it was like the bulging trunk of a tree above them, ten times their own height.

Then they saw the first hind leg, which must have been quite twelve feet from the tail tip. It was like a crocodile's hind leg and, like the tail, it was fully scaled, and furnished with curved pale claws, each as long as a gnome!

You might well think that the gnomes, having seen what it was, would have been well advised to investigate no further. But the truth is, the gnomes

were very inquisitive creatures, and possessed plenty of pluck too; they felt they *had* to see the whole of this creature, however big and fearsome it was.

So they crept on, under the vast scaled body, past the fearsome back claws, along towards the head.

When Lobgob looked upwards he could not see the actual back of the dragon (for, of course, that is exactly what the creature was). To do that he would have had to climb a tall ladder.

If he had done so he would have seen a scalloped frill of hard skin, like a keel, or the back fin of a fish, which grew out of the centre of the back. This was brilliant green in colour. All Lobgob could see was the huge barrel-like body overhanging him, covered all over (laminated is the term) with very hard shiny scales which were polished like the scales of a fish. The body, like the tail, was a greenish blue, though the tummy was silvery white and not so shiny.

Then came the front legs, each toe tipped with a pale curving claw of razor sharpness and then, at last, the head. It was a most fearsome head.

Of course, long, long ago in the Forest of Boland there had been dragons, one or two. Hal o' the Hobb, who was well over a thousand years old, remembered tales passed down from his great-great-grandfather of the dragons which lived in the Forest. These fairy-tales always made out that the dragons were not horrible or dangerous at all, but kindly, clumsy creatures, which lived on herbs, grass, and the foliage of bushes and trees. They were on friendly terms with the gnomes who also lived in the Forest, and they even spoke a sort of 'pigeon gnome' language which could be understood.

Perhaps Lobgob, remembering these tales which he had heard many times when he was a gombie, was less afraid. But I must say, to look at that great sleeping head was enough to scare the boldest heart.

It was about the size of an elephant's head, but of course longer in shape. It had two rather curious ears, sticking straight up like the pricked ears of a horse, and seeming far too small in comparison with the rest; these were lined inside with coarse hair. The face and snout were scaled, the eyelids, which were closed, had long straw-coloured lashes. The dragon seemed to be fast asleep, breathing as regularly as a babe, with perhaps the faint suggestion of a smile on its face.

The gnomes grew very bold now; they walked all around the head (without of course daring to touch it, or making a noise). They walked all round and down the far side of the recumbent body.

And still the dragon slept.

Hal o' the Hobb, who, like Bumbletummy, the Station-Master at Boland Banks, was busy in his garden that bright morning, was startled to hear in the distance the frantic hoarse puffings of the Boland Belle. It was unusual for the engine to return at this time of day; indeed, it was against all regulations as laid down by the Railway Company. Hal knew at once something was amiss.

Hastily he threw down his spade and reached for

his leather coat, and as he hurried down the path to the Station he saw the white smoke from the funnel of the Boland Belle drifting through the trees.

Disregarding the signal which was against it (actually, I'm afraid the signalman, whose name was Snoutgrass, had gone up to the village to post a letter – strictly against the rules, of course), the engine came rocking round the bend with Lobgob leaning out of the cab, waving frantically.

He pulled the locomotive up at the platform with a squeal of brakes and clouds of steam and came running to tell Hal the alarming news. Up at Boland Banks wombies and gombies were clustered at their doors, shielding their eyes from the glare of the sun. They, like Hal, were completely mystified. The rumours flew that there had been an accident at the mine and someone sent for Lock 'Em Up Loopy, the village policeman, who came puffing out of his house struggling into his uniform coat, a blue jacket with large bright buttons made of silver. At one period of his career he had been relieved of his job, but had now wangled it back again.

Soon everyone who could run, walk, hobble, or toddle was converging on the Station to find out what it was all about. But before they could reach the platform the engine started up again with Hal on board, and away it went, backwards, down the line.

Lock 'Em Up Loopy was left behind, which made him very angry. He had great ideas of his own importance, and it maddened him to think that Hal had left without him. He vented his feelings on the rabble of wombies and gombies who came pouring through the station gate.

'Be off, all of ye!' he roared. 'Be off to your houses this instant or 'twill be the worse for you. And the first person who asks me what's happened will go into the Lock-Up.'

Well, as I think you'll agree, Hal found a problem on his hands when he reached the mine at Poolewe! It's perfectly true that the dragon was still sleeping, as peacefully as a babe, but what was to prevent its waking up? Mind you, the dragon would not have harmed the gnomes, not for the world. By all accounts they had always been friendly to the little people in days gone by, and this was a very good-natured dragon indeed, whose favourite diet, when he used to roam the Forest of Boland many centuries before, had been the lower leaves of trees such as sallow and willow. But all the same, if he *did* make up his mind to wake up and venture forth to explore all his old haunts, then he might do a considerable amount of damage, as you may well guess.

There was the railway, for instance, with all its little junctions, stations and signal-boxes, and the miles of railway lines so truly laid.

With that great bulk turned loose there was no knowing what would happen! Even if it were possible to reason with the creature, it couldn't stir very far without causing a great deal of damage.

As long as it continued to slumber so peacefully all would be well. Even that rich seam of gold must wait. If they started quarrying it, the noise might wake the dragon.

All the same, Hal was not quite happy in his mind about the business, though he took care to make light of his anxieties and kept his private opinions to himself.

3

WIZARD WIZARDRY

WIZARD HOMM sat at the door of his cave on the hill. Ding, Dong and Belle were chewing the fragile bones of a weasel close to the three-legged stool on which the Wizard sat and the minute crunching noises were rather distracting.

It was a hot afternoon towards the end of June. The heavy air smelt thick and sweet, like the atmosphere of a greenhouse. Wizard Homm was in a bad temper. It may have been due to the heat, and the fact that most of his spells had gone wrong lately. For instance, the peasants wanted rain. Three times a week one or another of them would come toiling up from the village, asking Homm to send rain for the crops, and there was no sign of it. And another thing, what about the spell he put on pretty little Helda? That was three months ago. Nothing had happened. Every time he went down into the village he caught sight of her playing happily about with the other village children, and he did his best to avoid her.

Wizard Homm looked out over the valley which shook and danced in the heat. The distant trees were muffled in haze, the cultivated ground near the village, which was fenced round with wattle palings in an effort to keep the Forest animals at bay, was no longer a lush bright green. Now it glowed brown. The wheat was stunted and parched. If this drought went on, Wizard Homm would be laughed at by the villagers and they would no longer bring him their pieces of silver – not a pleasant prospect!

He got up from his three-legged stool, and gathering his midnight-blue gown about him, he strode into the cave, fumbling for his spectacles, for Wizard or no Wizard, his sight was not so good as it was. Just inside the entrance was a bookcase full of books, all bound in leather and punctured with wormholes. There was a rough-hewn table, together with a chair, and all about were jars of herbs, boxes of skulls, bones (some human ones), and one or two vats of a bright purple liquid which looked like ink but wasn't.

Wizard Homm moved over to the pile of books and studied the titles on the backs of the huge leather tomes. Here are some of them:

Some Sorcerers' Sauces, Necromancy in a Month, Which Witch? (a thriller), *Spellbound, The Wizards' Cookery Book, Rainmaking Made Easy, Wizards and Warlocks, How to Disappear, Smells and Spells.*

Wizard Homm, after much deliberation, chose an enormous volume whose title was *Wizard Wizardry.*

Carrying this with some difficulty back to his three-legged stool, he placed it on his knees and adjusted his glasses. He wanted a new spell, one he hadn't tried before. Here was an interesting one.

How to Turn Little Girls into Wombats. (Just the thing for little Helda, he thought.)

Take of fat of a Moll Hern two drams, Mummy, finely powdered, two scruples, Camphire, Galbanum and Piscatorum Mirabile one gram, and of Dragon's Blood three drams. Mix well, according to art. Say you then as followeth:

> *Hoodlum Dee*
> *Hoodlum Do*
> *Hink 'Em, Bink 'Em,*
> *Bunkum Bo.*

'Pah! no good at all,' muttered Wizard Homm to himself, 'no Dragon's Blood. It's as bad as saying "take half a pound of butter and a pint of cream" when you haven't any. These books need bringing up to date.'

Wizard Homm hadn't the faintest idea what a Wombat was, or what it looked like, but it sounded nasty; he would have dearly liked to try it on little Helda.

Really — it was most annoying. Nearly all these recipes demanded Dragon's Blood. Perhaps that was why so many of his spells were so ineffective — one just couldn't get the stuff these days. One had to make shift with newts, frogs, efts, toads, bats, and snakes.

One thing was certain; if he didn't bring rain soon

there would be no money left in the big leather bag which was under his bracken mattress in the cave, and even Wizard Homm couldn't make gold or silver.

He was so busy over his big book that he didn't see a small toiling figure coming up the slope below, between the full-flowered elder bushes. Then Ding, Dong and Belle came running under the skirts of Homm's silver-starred gown. He looked up over his glasses. It was that man Halberd again, with the sweat running down off his nose.

He was a thickset, shock-haired fellow, clad in a faded blue jerkin and trousers of pyjama pattern, cross-gartered with leather thongs. These trousers were called 'braies' and were worn by all the peasantry in those parts.

The man stood there with hands clasped before him and with his eyes fixed on the hem of Wizard Homm's gown, where the circular bewhiskered faces of Ding, Dong and Belle poked out, glaring at him with their cruel, almond eyes.

'Well,' grunted Wizard Homm testily, 'what is it now, please?'

'High and mighty Wizard Homm, my corn is burning under this sun. Send us rain, Wizard Homm, send us rain in the valley tonight – tomorrow – or we will be ruined!'

'Your money?' asked Wizard Homm. 'Where is your money? I can't do anything without a higher fee. That's why I can't send you the rain. I'm raising my fees; even a Wizard must eat.'

'How much, Wizard Homm?' asked Halberd in a trembling voice. 'I'm only a poor peasant, as you well know.'

'Two crowns is the price,' said Wizard Homm at once. 'For two crowns you shall have rain, take it or leave it,' and he opened his big book as though, as far as he was concerned, the matter were ended.

'But when will it come, high and mighty Wizard? You told us last week we should have rain, but the sun still burns by day and there is no dew by night! If you will send it soon, I will indeed give you two crowns, though I shall have to go without my supper, and so will my wife and little Helda, my daughter!'

Wizard Homm knew there was only a single crown left in his own money bag. He would take a chance; besides, he liked the idea of little Helda going without her supper. 'For two crowns, my good man, you shall have rain tonight, before moonrise,' he added, rashly, to make it sound more convincing.

Halberd fumbled with a shaking hand in the leather purse he carried at his belt and passed over the money. 'You are very kind, high and mighty Wizard. Two crowns is a lot of money for a poor man like myself; but if the rain does not come, we shall starve next winter.'

Wizard Homm pocketed the crowns and turned again to his book. 'Be off with you now, my good man, I'm very busy.'

The Wizard watched Halberd getting smaller and smaller, as he went among the elder bushes. The sun

was lowering in the west, shadows were tracing cool fingers far across the meads, and from the Forest behind him the low continuous hum of insects seemed to be intensified.

I've stuck my neck out now, thought Wizard Homm. I must find a good working spell or, bejabers, my name will be a laughing-stock! He adjusted his spectacles again and turned the pages of his big book until he came to the Rs.

'R. (Here we are.) RAIN. *How to make.*

'*Recipe No. 1. Take you a frog's leg, tie in a leathern bag, boil in a pot with half-a-gill of Dragon's Blood* – Blow the thing!' ejaculated Wizard Homm, almost shutting the book in anger. 'There we go again, *Dragon's Blood!*

'Let's try another spell.

'*RAIN. Recipe No. 2. Take a catt. Cutt you off its tail, stew the tail in a gallipot with four drams of Epsom salts and of Periscara Tatara one scruple. Recite:*

> *Rain, rain, tummy pain,*
> *Sleep it off and start again.*'

Wizard Homm made a grab at Dong, who was still peeping out from under his gown, watching Halberd descend the hill. But the cat was too quick for him. It scuttled into the cave where it hid under Wizard Homm's bed. Ding and Belle, sensing trouble, wisely made themselves scarce.

'Let's see if there's another . . .

'RAIN. How to attract. Recipe No. 3. *Take you two leaves of Snoreweed, add two fried spiders and the blunt end of a dew-worm. Bury the same under an oak tree and wish.*'

That sounded simple enough. He wouldn't have the trouble of catching Dong to cut off his tail. Snoreweed was a sinister plant which grew sparingly in marshy places, both in the Forest itself, and in the damp valleys nearby, where elder was to be found.

Curiously enough, Wizard Homm hadn't used snoreweed before, but he'd heard about it. The peasants gave it to their children (in minute quantities, of course) when they had the toothache or when they were restless with the measles. It was pretty potent; if you took too much it sent you to sleep for long periods – sometimes you never woke up again.

Wizard Homm carefully straightened his tall black hat, and grasping his knotted staff, on which were carved serpents entwined, he set off down the slope for the elder thickets. There the grass was cool, long, and green. Cottonrod rabbits gambolled about, the strange wild scent of the flat yellow elder flowers drenched the air, midges danced.

After a good deal of searching he found what he wanted, a clump of snoreweed growing under an elder bush. The leaves were rather like those of a laurel, with sharp points to their tips. The underside was quite silvery and silky.

The Wizard put them carefully into his bag. This

was indeed a lucky find; he would make the spell as soon as he got back to his cave.

Wizard Homm, peering at the Rain recipe through his thick-rimmed glasses, mixed the snoreweed leaves, the spiders, and the blunt end of a dew-worm very carefully. Then he made a small excavation at the foot of the big oak near the mouth of his cave, buried the mixture, and duly wished his wish. When he had finished this important task he sat down on his stool, wrapt in contemplation.

The sun had set by now. The heavy, thick, stillness of the atmosphere seemed to be intensified. Down in the valley the blue wood-smoke from the huts rose up straight into the upper air where it spread out in a blue veil, quite level, like a ceiling of gossamer. From where he sat Wizard Homm could smell the elder flowers very strongly. Behind him the Forest was deathly still.

Ding, Dong and Belle returned stealthily from their various places of concealment for they sensed the danger of losing their tails had passed. They came rubbing back and forth against the Wizard's leather boots with their sensitive tails straight up in the air, making noises like tiny throbbing motor bikes.

The valley darkened. Owls began to hoot mournfully. Wizard Homm stared at the brooding, thick Forest which came within a hundred yards of his cave. He wondered what lay far back in those hidden thickets.

The Boland Water brook, which flowed close to the village in the valley, entered the Forest below the hill, but no man had ever followed its course either on foot or by boat. He could see the bright thread of water, shrunk by the drought and bushed in by willows and alders, twisting and looping its way through the green meadows before it boldly entered the trees.

Even though he was a Wizard the Forest was a closed book to him, for no man, not even a great and powerful Wizard, ventured there. It is true that in the autumn, when gathering firewood, he entered it, just within the margins, but nothing would induce him to explore further. Yet in some strange way he felt drawn to it, like a twig to the lip of a waterfall.

In summer, it seemed more mysterious than ever, when all the leaves were so thick and green.

Being a Wizard, Homm did not often feel lonely, nor did he wish to mingle with the men of the valley; anyhow, the peasants couldn't even read, or carry on an intelligent conversation.

Occasionally, it is true, some great noble, or the Lord Boland, who lived nearby, would come riding up the hill attended by his retinue of servants. Usually it was with the request to send rain, a wife, an heir, or something of that sort. Such visits meant a period of prosperity to the Wizard for he was paid handsomely with bags of gold.

Wizard Homm was cunning. He always told them that he would do his best, but if a daughter arrived instead of a son then this meant that he had been underpaid. The whole business was purely commercial. As the chances of a son were fifty-fifty, Wizard Homm made a good thing out of it.

When a son *did* arrive, as it was bound to do at times, then the Wizard's fame was spread far and wide by delighted clients. A successful result meant a good season for Wizard Homm. The only trouble was that there were very few nobles in the countryside, and those who did come, had to ride many a long and weary league. Because it was unthinkable to ride *through* the Forest, they had to go round it.

As the Wizard sat there he noticed a subtle change coming over the breathless stillness of the scene before him.

A sudden breeze puffed in the folds of his star-bespangled gown, a soft sigh passed through the leaves of the spreading oak overhead.

Then a great blackness came gradually swelling out of the west, and the sleeping Forest began to murmur, a deep, low, rushing murmur, like the distant voice of the vast sea.

Then – a muttering of thunder; far away, a vivid

snoreweed

flash flickered and was gone. Wizard Homm began to be excited. This latest spell with the snoreweed seemed to be working at last! It was about time he had a break.

Ding, Dong and

Belle scuttled under the hem of his gown, always a sign that something was amiss. A heavy cool drop of rain, like a pellet of cold lead, smote him on his hand. Another rattled on his tall black hat. The next moment the torrent came drumming and roaring on the leaves, driving the Wizard post-haste into the shelter of his cave, with his flowing garment gathered up to his knees like a dressing-gown.

Soon the roar of the rain drowned the thunder and a great wind raved in the Forest of Boland; a sound quite terrifying, a deep booming roar which grew, retreated, and came again. The oak branches were swept upwards, the leaves showing their pale undersides, and very soon water was running in great twisted ropes, like barley sugar, from the rim of the cave mouth.

Even the Wizard, in all his uncountable years in his lonely cave, had never seen or heard rain like this. It came down in a close forest of silver rods; when it hit the ground it rebounded in a dense spray.

Down in the village the peasants cowered under their thatch, quite terrified. Halberd, hugging his wife and little Helda close, shivered in his shoes, not so much at the fury of the storm but at the dreadful power of Wizard Homm.

'He's overdone it this time!' the poor man groaned aloud. 'All the geese will swim away, our crops will be flat tomorrow. Truly he is a mighty Wizard!'

In the Forest of Boland, many miles distant, the

Boland Water (the stream which traversed the Forest from end to end) rose every hour until the broad waters flooded out among the roots of the trees. The trestle bridges, built by the gnomes at Poolewe and at Boland Water Station on the other branch line, trembled under the pressure of the flood and one by one the timber supports, built with so much labour, toppled and were swept away, tossing and rearing like cabers in the red flood.

At Poolewe the water came rushing in a turgid torrent into the mouth of the new mine. It came swirling into the darkness where the dragon was sleeping, it washed along his plated sides, creeping higher and higher.

The poor old dragon was having a fearful dream. His legs began to make running motions, like those of a slumbering dog, his great lips curled back, he uttered strange muffled squeaks and grunts. Soon the water was half-way up his back and lapping his nostrils.

With one gigantic sneeze, which seemed to shake the mine to its utmost crannies, the dragon opened his eyes. His huge nostrils began to smoke and steam like kettles. Nothing like this had ever happened before.

From time to time there had been great floods down the endless years, but deep in his sealed cave he had been secure.

He rose unsteadily to his short legs and shook himself like a stupendous dog. Then splashing, roaring, hissing, and steaming, he turned round and half-lumbering, half-swimming with powerful sweeps of his scaly tail, he made his way towards the mouth of the mine.

4

A NASTY SITUATION

WIZARD HOMM had certainly worked a powerful spell. Nobody was more conscious of the fact than the Wizard himself. In a very short while he saw, to his astonishment, the spring, that normally fell in a silver whisper among the ferns outside his cave magnified into a red-brown torrent which came tumbling and roaring, closer and closer to the entrance.

Soon it was beginning to trickle in over the threshold. The Wizard knew he would have to act quickly. No amount of work with spade or broom would keep the encroaching waters at bay, only a counter-spell would do the trick.

The trouble was, that by the time Wizard Homm

awoke to this fact, his bed in the corner of the cave was beginning to float, the wooden legs bumping gently now and then 'dunk . . . dunk' on the stone floor. His table would soon be floating too. The three cats, spitting and swearing, and with very anxious expressions on their round bewhiskered faces, were seeking refuge on top of the bookcase which, weighted by its leather tomes, had not yet begun to move.

And would you believe it? Wizard Homm had lost the book of spells, the valuable volume entitled *Wizard Wizardry*! He was sure he put it back on the shelf after he had finished with it, but search how he might he couldn't see it, the reason being that he couldn't find his glasses; he'd laid them down somewhere, and no doubt the waters had hidden them!

As he peered and scrabbled, holding a rushlight high above his head, he felt a stealthy icy coldness, a wetness, slowly rising up his legs. Then his wooden bedstead, which was now voyaging around the rocky chamber, took him in the back of the knees and down went Wizard Homm into the water!

As a matter of fact this proved a blessing in disguise. As he landed in a sitting position on the floor of the cave, his frantic groping fingers encountered the precious spectacle case. He was able (with some difficulty) to wipe them clean and get to his feet. Luckily he had managed to hold his rush candle clear of the wet, even when he sat down so unexpectedly, and he now returned by a circuitous route to the bookcase, which was still aground, and in a moment he saw the book he was after – *Wizard Wizardry*.

He carried it to the table, climbed the latter to weight it down, and with fevered haste turned the pages.

'R. RAIN. *How to stop it.* Here we are.

'*Recipe No.* 1. *Take the gut of a cuttle-fish, mix with it two cloves and an ounce of Dragon's Blood . . .*'

Wizard Homm gave a snort of impatience. How on earth was he to get hold of the gut of a cuttle-fish, or Dragon's Blood for that matter?

'*Recipe No.* 2. (Ah! this is better. Here's our old friend snoreweed again.)

'*To make Rain to Cease. Take you the bones of a mouse powdered, the left eye of a Natterjack Toad, put in a Stoppered Jar and place therin a Leaf of Snoreweed (crushed). Cover with Water and pronounce these words:*

Watersmeet, Watersmeet, Meet Your Match
Keep Away From My Nice Thatch.
Hubbly Bubbly, Past My Door,
Treble Chance And a Family Four.'

The words were quite unintelligible to Wizard Homm, but what did that matter?

He had, most luckily, the ingredients to hand, for he kept all kinds of charms and oddments in big stoppered jars on an upper shelf and he had taken

the precaution to lay in a goodly reserve of snore-weed which was now hanging by a string from the ceiling.

It was a horrible business, slip-slopping about in the still rising water, but he managed to work the spell and say the magic words, though by that time he was standing on his stool with his draggled blue gown pulled well up about his hairy knobbly knees.

The three cats had sought greater safety in the roof of the cave. The trouble was, the Wizard didn't know how long it would take the spell to work – if it did work. He watched the water slip-slopping about his toes with great anxiety. If it went on rising he'd have to get out of the cave and climb to higher ground.

But as soon as the spell was made, and the magic words were spoken, the dull drumming roar outside the cave gradually eased away until all was silent save for the 'drip! drop! tink! tonk!' of water drops falling from the rocks, ferns, and pieces of furniture. And, most heartening of all, the water began to fall inch by inch, like a retreating tide.

Wizard Homm was soon able to step off his stool and get busy with his birch-wood broom, sweeping the water out of the cave. As he worked he reflected that, after all, discovering this new and powerful weed had almost been worth it. It seemed to work every time.

Ding, Dong, and Belle came down from the roof in easy stages, first to the top of the bookcase, then to the bed, which had now gone aground, then to the floor where they at once scampered outside, into the fresh air.

But the whole place was in a fearful mess. It would take *days* to dry out, and there was certainly no spell in the book to tell you how to dry out Wizards' caves.

By dawn the little streamlet was again whispering and silvery among its ferns, but the valley presented a sorry sight. The floods had ravaged the village; they had swept, feet deep, through the wattle houses and several of the peasants' oxen had been borne away on the flowing stream, the Boland Water, which entered the Forest half a mile distant.

The Wizard stood at his cave mouth regarding the havoc wrought during the night and he felt a glow of pride within himself. 'That'll teach 'em,' he said aloud, 'that'll show 'em I'm a Wizard not to be trifled with! Now I expect they'll come whining for sun. Yes, by my tall hat! Here comes the first one, and it's that fellow Halberd again, punting across on a table top.'

Wizard Homm began to laugh so much at the sight of the poor peasant that he almost fell over. But then he remembered it was undignified for a Wizard to laugh. He sat down on his stool and tried to look as imposing and as dry as possible, which wasn't easy as his blue gown was steaming in the hot sun.

Halberd crossed the flood with difficulty and began to climb the hill. He looked like a half-drowned rat.

'How now Halberd?' The Wizard looked sternly

at the poor fellow who had fallen on his knees before him.

'O mighty, most mighty Wizard Homm, you have been to generous with your rain! Alas! my crops have been washed away, and two of my oxen, they have been swept into the Forest. But most dreadful thing of all, we've lost our little Helda! She was washed away from her mother's arms when the flood struck our house! She's been carried on the bosom of the flood into the dark Forest clinging to a pig trough. O Wizard Homm, we shall never see her again, not unless you make a spell to bring her back to us! My oxen, my geese, my crops, my wife, my home are as nothing, but our little Helda, ah! she is all we had, she was our life, our joy. Now she has been taken from us by the cruel waters. Please, please, Wizard Homm, bring her back to us!'

Wizard Homm was secretly astonished at the turn of events. Evidently the former spell he put upon little Helda had worked as well; he really had 'killed two birds with one stone', as they say.

'Well, well, my good man, you asked for rain and I sent it – you never said how much you wanted. As for your child, why worry? I'll make a spell to send you another, a lusty son this time, if you wish, who will help you with the harvest and till your fields. That is,' the Wizard added, as an after-thought, 'if I am paid my fee, of course.'

'Fee!' gasped poor Halberd, sitting back on his heels, 'but Wizard Homm you have taken everything from us: my money, such as I had, my all!'

'Then you must start again, till your fields anew,' replied the Wizard cheerfully and most unfeelingly. 'I'll see you have good growing weather. Tut! tut! man, don't take on so. Your daughter could never have helped you with your work, daughters are only an encumbrance. Count yourself lucky to be rid of her!'

A change came over Halberd. He ceased to sob wildly. He stood up, the water still dripping from his jerkin and trousers. He was no longer the weeping submissive peasant; his face was twisted with hate and anguish.

'Then you're a wicked old Wizard!' he shouted. 'You've ruined me, as you've ruined everyone else in the village. What our little Helda said was true, you're a nasty old whiskery Wizard, and we'd be better off without you! Go on!' he shouted as Wizard Homm rose with awful calm from his stool. 'I'm not afraid of you – turn me into a frog, or a cotton-rod rabbit, anything you like, but now you know the truth. If I *do* get back to the valley I'll raise the whole lot of them against you. We'll come back and smoke you out, we'll cut off your head and hang it up for the hawks to pick at! So now you know!'

Then, without another word, Halberd turned about and strode away down the hill never looking back.

'Here's a nice kettle of fish,' said Wizard Homm to himself. It would never do to let Halberd get away with this piece of impertinence. He certainly *would* turn him into a frog, if he could.

But by the time the Wizard had grabbed *Wizard Wizardry* and found the right page Halberd was across the flood and back inside his house.

To tell you the truth, Wizard Homm was quite overcome by the potency of his new spells. There was no doubt at all that the snoreweed was responsible. He had never had results like this before. It pleased him mightily to think little Helda had been swept away into the Forest and he hoped that would be the last of her. It looked as though his first spell had worked after all. Now he could go down to the village to do his weekly shopping without fear of ridicule; indeed, it would surprise him if he were not treated with much increased respect and bigger payments in gold.

All the same, he couldn't stand for this latest outburst of temper on the part of little Helda's father. He certainly must not be allowed to get away with it.

'Let's see,' said Wizard Homm aloud to his cats, 'if we can find something really nasty for Mr Halberd.'

He fetched the big book again and sat down on his stool. The sun had come out and the whole valley was steaming after the flood. Herons were stalking about where poor Halberd's crops once flourished, catching frogs no doubt. Perhaps it would be best to turn Halberd into an eft, then the herons would gobble him up.

The Wizard thumbed the pages over. Some of the writing was in Latin. On every page were diagrams, stars, horoscopes, and the like. But it was only those spells which required snoreweed which interested him; it seemed almost as good as Dragon's Blood from all accounts.

'Ah!' exclaimed Wizard Homm, stroking his long beard, 'here we are, page 203. *To Turn a Man into an Eft.*

'*Take you a leaf of Snoreweed, mix with it three Jelly Babies and crushed bone buttons from m' tutor's trousers, add one scruple of Dragon's Blood (O bother!) and stir well for an hour with the Femur of a Bittern.*'

Pah! An impossible recipe! For one thing he hadn't any trouser buttons belonging to m' tutor, or a leg bone of a bittern, and of course he had no Dragon's Blood. Nearly every recipe mentioned the stuff. The book was clearly out of date.

Never mind, he hadn't done so badly. Later on, he'd go down to the village and fill his shopping basket.

But in a very short while something happened which made the Wizard change his mind. He had just finished an excellent breakfast of hens' eggs and cold boiled bacon, and the cats had finished the rind, when he noticed people gathering, like angry wasps, down in the village. Men were running from door to door, women were collecting in knots with their heads together, and soon the reason for these ominous preparations was made plain. The peasants were assembling, *arming themselves with spears, hay*

forks, and clubs, and led by Halberd, they began to stream over the muddy plain towards the foot of his hill.

Now it must be admitted, this was a very nasty situation. There was certainly no time to make any magic. After all, it takes time for a spell to work, sometimes it's a matter of hours; there was nothing the Wizard could do about a sudden emergency like this.

Had he been more powerful, things might have been different, he might have even disappeared. Wizard Homm thought quickly. When the peasants arrived thirsting for his blood (for they certainly looked like business), they must find the cave empty and the bird flown, as the saying is.

He grabbed his staff and the big leather book – without that he would be truly lost – and, calling his cats, he sneaked into the trees behind the cave.

He planned to go only a little way into the Forest and hide, where perhaps he would have time to work a spell to bring another deluge.

The Wizard clambered over the rocks, pushing aside the trailing creepers of ivy, and plunged into the cool green bracken which came almost to his shoulders. The three cats ran after him, in the manner of all cats, tails erect, and with frequent stops and sudden darts. Sometimes they ran on ahead and played peep bo! round the roots of the ferns; sometimes they ran up the trees and hung there half-way up, like playful squirrels.

As the angry and determined peasants climbed

the hill, they made a great noise, partly to keep up their spirits and partly to intimidate the Wizard. They were certainly successful on both counts. When the Wizard heard those hoarse wild shouts, he knew that he would be given no mercy, once he fell into their hands; they would beat him to a pulp.

Soon his dignified walk became a trot, his trot a run. The briars tore at his blue gown, they ripped across the backs of his scraggy hands until the pale blood flowed, they wrapped themselves around his knobbly knees. For the first time in his life he was afraid. Though he was becoming puffed with his exertions he never let go of his big book.

The cats thought it a great joke.

I don't know how long he continued in his mad career, but when at last he sank down among the ferns he was quite exhausted, even though he was a Wizard, and he knew he could go no farther. The perils of the Forest were not so great as the recent danger. He had penetrated so far into the thickets that all sounds of pursuit had died; he didn't hear the crackling of the flames as the peasants set fire to all his sticks of furniture, his table, his bed, and his wicked books, skulls and bones. Nor did he smell the acrid smoke which hung over the sodden valley in an avenging veil.

But one thing he well knew: it would be most unwise to return to his cave while the peasants remained in the valley.

5

DRAGON'S BLOOD

WIZARD HOMM lay a long time in the tall bracken; he lay so long that soon it was late afternoon and the sun had passed around the sky. It shone down upon him through the gaps in the oak leaves and all he had for company were his cats and his big book of magic.

He watched the midges dancing up and down, he listened to the small rustles in the green fern, he watched the busy journeyings of spiders, beetles, woodlice, caterpillars, and long-legged flies, and all the time he listened for sounds which would tell him he was being followed. But all was peace.

Then he remembered that he'd made a very foolish mistake – he'd forgotten to bring any snoreweed with him. The Wizard well knew he could only find this weed in special places. Well, he thought, I certainly shan't get anywhere just lying here! I wonder, he said to himself, I wonder, if I could sneak back to my cave after dark?

That was all very well, but he wasn't quite sure which way he had come. The Wizard was no hand at tracking.

And what a weight this great book was, to be

sure! Still, he'd done the wise thing in bringing it.

He got to his feet and began to retrace his steps, or so he thought, in the direction of the outskirts of the Forest. He was feeling very hungry. Perhaps he'd have to eat the cats. They seemed to be enjoying themselves well enough, for it was quite an outing for them. They were frisking about, and darting up trees as merrily as ever, and they had all dined well, for whilst the Wizard had been hiding in the bracken they had caught plenty of wood mice. Their exuberant joy was irritating – if they weren't careful he'd change them into something else, ladybirds perhaps.

'I'm sure I recognize that tree,' said the Wizard to himself, when he reached a turn in the path, 'another step or two and I shall see the Forest beginning to thin and I shall be out of this horrid place.'

But it wasn't the same tree. A little farther on, he was sure he remembered seeing a big boulder which stood under a yew tree.

But it wasn't, you know.

Wizard Homm was lost, and with every step, he was getting deeper and deeper into the great Forest of Boland! And another thing. Night would soon be upon him. Already the shadows lay long across the ridings and only the tops of the oaks were lit by the declining rays.

After wandering for another hour or so the Wizard heard a sound which gave him great hope. It was the gurgle of a stream. Now, if once he could find the Boland Water, that would be a sure path; it would lead him out of the Forest, a silver thread to safety. He had only to follow it up, in the opposite direction to the flow of the water, and it would bring him out at his cave.

But when he came upon the stream he saw it was half the size of the Boland Water, so that didn't help him much! All the same, it *was* water, a pretty babbling brooklet, and a small stream is always company, almost as good as a dog.

Moreover, Wizard Homm was very thirsty. Forgetting all about his fine blue gown he threw himself down among the water mints, and holding his long beard well out of the way with one hand he had a long, long drink.

The clear cold water was delicious. The Wizard was soon feeling much refreshed. And he was more pleased still when, after following the stream for another mile or so, he found it was becoming wider and the Forest more open and rocky. There were signs now of the havoc of the recent floods (*his* floods, or so he liked to think); huge trees uprooted and aground on the dry shingle and lines of rubbish, dead sticks, grass and so forth, caught up in the lower branches of the thickets where the raging muddy waters had scoured a passage.

So the flood had reached this far! Wizard Homm chuckled. 'I certainly made a wonderful, powerful magic. I'm the mightiest of all Wizards, and the sooner I find some more snoreweed the better!' (he said to himself).

All sounds of birds had died away now. There was

only the babbling of the stream to keep him company and, of course, his cats. The sun had gone, the sky over the tops of the oaks was mellow and tranquil. Suddenly Ding, Dong and Belle came running under the skirts of his blue gown. Wizard Homm stood motionless, clasping his big book.

He was on a deer path which was well above the meandering stream so that he could look down upon it as it sparkled and gurgled among its polished stones. Round the next bend there were strange sounds, a regular tearing, scrunching noise, and from time to time loud rumbles, like muffled thunder. The tops of some willows down by the brook were being violently shaken. Wizard Homm was quite mystified!

He was also a little scared; the cats certainly were, for he could feel them warm, furry and trembling, against his briar-scratched legs.

Very cautiously the Wizard advanced through the bracken, and peeping over the edge of the bank he saw a sight which momentarily turned his heart to water.

There, quietly browsing among the willows and sallows close to the bank of the stream, was *an enormous dragon*! It was reaching up its long neck and chewing off the tops of the bushes. From time to time its scaly tummy gave forth prodigious rumbles. It seemed very hungry, and though it was of terrifying size its pale, long eyelashes and good-natured face seemed to show it was quite a peaceable sort of creature. But you can't always rely on appearances.

Bears look cuddly enough; actually, as you may know, they are treacherous and fierce. This was certainly the first dragon the Wizard had ever seen – indeed he hadn't the foggiest idea that there were any dragons left in the Forest of Boland!

Now as he lay secretly watching it an ugly idea was born in the mind of this wicked Wizard! Didn't his big book say that Dragon's Blood was absolutely the finest thing you could have with which to make a spell?

Nearly all the recipes in his huge leather-bound book mentioned it! If he could, by some means, slay this dragon, then he would have the power to do anything he wanted, within reason (and out of it). He could turn Halberd into an eft as easily as you could put on your hat, or he could make himself invisible in next to no time, just like it said in his book *How to Disappear*. He had some of the recipes by heart and nearly every one required Dragon's Blood.

But it took some thinking out. Even if you happen to be a Wizard, you can't fight dragons unless you have special spells and a good suit of armour, to say nothing of a sword, shield, and possibly a couple of spears.

Meanwhile, as all these ugly thoughts were passing through the Wizard's mind, the poor unsuspecting old dragon was making a hearty meal. After all, we must remember it had been cooped up in a cave for donkey's years, so no wonder it was hungry! So it ate, and ate, and all the time the sky over the oak

tops glowed more softly and the little stream gurgled on as though browsing dragons were all in the day's work.

Then the Wizard noticed that a little way along the path there was a big polished boulder standing on the very lip of the slope.

Now, thought Wizard Homm, if I can manage to push this boulder down on top of the dragon, I'd very likely do it in.

It was an ingenious way out of a difficulty. Wizard Homm determined to try it. Very cautiously he crept along the bank until he was behind the big stone. The dragon was slowly feeding along the willows and coming towards him. It raised its head and stared towards the bank behind which Wizard Homm was lying in wait.

Its eyesight was not very good but once it *did* see something peeping over the willows – a round black stove-pipe object (which was of course the Wizard's hat). It stared at it for some seconds but then the black object disappeared and the dragon thought no more about it and went on feeding.

Nearer and nearer it waddled, but its progress was agonizingly slow. Now and again it would stop tearing off the leaves (which it seemed to shear off as easily as an electric hedge-cutter) and waddle down to the stony bank and take a long draught of water.

It drank like a gigantic cow with its muzzle in the stream, sucking and gulping, and, now and then, lifting its long neck and letting the silver drops dribble off its chin hairs on to the stones beside the brook.

At last the dragon was directly below Wizard Homm. So he got his shoulder to the great stone, he heaved and shoved with all his might, he grunted and pushed, he pushed and grunted.

At first it only rocked, for of course it had been well embedded in the bank for many years, and only the recent floods had weakened its hold.

But with one last prodigious heave the Wizard at last felt the great stone stir in its bed and poise for its final plunge. Very, very slowly it heeled over; the next moment, with an appalling roar and rumble it descended the bank, snapping off saplings as it fell and tearing up the bracken and the briars, bounding downwards like a huge grey football.

The poor old dragon was taken unawares – everything happened so quickly, though luckily it heard the onrush from above, and instinct made it turn its head. For all that, the great rock struck it a glancing blow on its big camel-like nose.

Now even a dragon can't take a bang on the nose like that without a certain amount of discomfort. Of course, if it had been a smaller creature it would probably have been killed then and there, but, as it was, the only result was that its nose bled. For some minutes it bled very badly. The poor old dragon was in a bit of a daze. It milled around, whisking its huge scaly tail like an enraged crocodile, sending the bushes flying like matchsticks. It was a good thing the Wizard wasn't at the foot of the bank.

It roared so loudly and so long with pain that the ground shook. Even the gnomes, away at Boland Banks, heard the uproar and guessed that the dragon had come out of the cave. They ran for their cross-bows and spears and Lock 'Em Up Loopy hurried off to get into his uniform and to find his truncheon – though their weapons would have been useless for dealing with a full-grown dragon.

After snorting and roaring and shaking its head a good deal from side to side, the poor old thing took to the water, which was quite deep just there. The Wizard, crouching in the bracken, and shivering in his shoes, saw it half-swim, half-paddle away until the trees hid it from view, and wasn't he glad to see it go!

The Wizard lay for quite a time, keeping quite still and watching the clouds of Dragon's Blood un-furling in the clear current like blue smoke. Then, as quick as a weasel, despite his long robe (which was now sadly torn by briars), Wizard Homm slithered down the steep bank and landed with a bump on the shingle.

From his waistcoat pocket he produced a small bottle which contained some useless concoction of his own, a cure for indigestion. This was quickly poured away. For here, if he was quick about it, was Dragon's Blood, the very stuff for making spells with! And it really *was* magical, as you will very soon see, far better than snoreweed, for instance.

But the Wizard had to be quick. Most of it had already sunk into the shingle and the sand. It was not red in colour, by the way, but a bright turquoise blue. Wizard Homm, by a careful search among the stones, managed to obtain about two tablespoonfuls of the precious stuff. He corked it up with great satisfaction and climbed again to the top of the bank. The cats had been so scared at the terrible goings-on that they had fled up a larch tree and for a long time wouldn't come down.

Wizard Homm didn't waste much time. He felt hungry, very hungry indeed, for he hadn't had anything to eat since his interrupted breakfast; and if he'd been without the Dragon's Blood I think he would have eaten his cats, if he could have caught them – which I doubt.

He sat down under an oak tree and quickly turned over his book of spells with a shaking finger. He soon found what he wanted without any trouble at all, a simple enough spell – *For Providing Supper. Of Dragon's Blood two scruples, of crushed elder flowers one minim and a cat's whisker.* He had some difficulty in obtaining the last, but he managed to grab Ding just as the cat was rubbing itself against his legs. Then he made his spell.

Almost at once a misty cloud began to form in the air in front of him. It was rather like a vague ball of fog which writhed about and turned on itself like tobacco smoke imprisoned under an upturned glass.

Then the writhing, twisting forms took shape and at the same time quite delicious smells assailed the hungry Wizard's nose so that his mouth began to tickle and saliva dribbled down his long beard.

A moment later the coiling fog faded. There, in front of him, was a small oak table of the kind that is known as rustic 'garden' furniture. It was spread with a clean white cloth embroidered at the hem with forget-me-nots and stars and a large H worked in blue silk. On the table was a plate. Upon it was a most appetizing mixed grill of three sausages, two eggs, ham, tomatoes, and kidneys, all piping hot, accompanied by crisp bread rolls warm from the oven, and a tall pewter tankard beside which stood a couple of bottles labelled 'Boland Ale'.

Wizard Homm soon polished off this delicious meal. He had barely laid down his knife and fork when there appeared yet another plate on which reposed a block of pink-and-white ice cream in which was stuck two wafers and a little wooden spoon to eat it with.

The Wizard gobbled the lot. Then, before he had time to wipe his beard, this plate vanished too, and there before him was a variety of cheeses, Danish Blue, Gorgonzola, a whole ripe Stilton wrapped in a white cloth, a red Dutch cheese, and a glass of Old Tawny Port.

But the Wizard had eaten so much he couldn't take any more on board, and just when he was thinking how nice it would be to have a smoke, the cheese disappeared and in its place was a box of the finest Havana cigars and a tin of tobacco.

The Wizard fumbled in his inner pockets and produced a gnarled, curved pipe. He had hardly filled it with tobacco when a lighted match appeared,

hovering over the bowl. The Wizard took it somewhat gingerly and lit his pipe. Then with a deep sigh
of content he leant back against the tree to enjoy
his after-dinner smoke.

As he did so, the rustic table with the remains
of his meal gradually faded until all he could see
before him was the tobacco tin. For some reason this
took longer to disappear. It hung before him, apparently suspended in mid air until it, too, melted like
snow in the sun, and everything was as it was before
he had made his spell; the green forest, the running
stream and the motionless willows. There was no
sound of the dragon, only the low murmur of the
stream and a night bird calling somewhere. Truly,
Dragon's Blood was just the job. Wizard Homm was
in luck at last, it seemed.

6

NEW FRIENDS
AND AN OLD ENEMY

Now you may well be wondering what happened
to the goose-girl, pretty little Helda.

You may remember that when the waters rose
and swamped the village, she had been carried away
down the stream clinging to her father's pig trough.
She had been swept on the breast of the flood, far
into the dark forest away from her beloved parents
and cackling geese.

What a frightening experience that was for her,
to be sure! How the waters swirled and raged in the
darkness, just like a horid dream. How scared she
was when she realized that she was being drawn
away into the tangled thickets and dark trees of the
Forest of Boland! Yet little Helda was very brave.
She clung to the pig trough with all her might and
main. There she stayed for I don't know how long as
the twirling, swirling, yellow waters bore her ever on.
Just when she was thinking that she could hold on
no longer and her fingers were becoming numb with
cold, the pig trough, which all this time had been
plunging and spinning, gave a hard jolt, then another, and at last came to a sudden stop on a bank
of shingle!

Little Helda dropped her toes. She felt gravel and the next moment was safe and sound among the green thickets of springing fern!

For some time she lay there recovering. Luckily for her the sun was rising and the shadows of night departing. She noticed also that the yellow flood was making less noise. When next she looked at the pig trough, which had been the means of saving her, she saw it was high and dry on the spotted stones. With every minute now the flood was sinking, just like a receding tide, and soon the stream would be its normal size.

And how beautiful the green forest appeared as the sun climbed higher in the sky! How rich were the smells of herbage, crushed water mint, bracken, oak and birch. Why did humans dread this beautiful forest? she thought.

She was very hungry, poor little girl. How was she to find any food? What had happened to her father and mother? Alas! She knew she had left them far behind outside the Forest. Had she been spared the flood to perish of starvation? She was sure she could never find her way back.

The warm rays of the sun streaming down through the openings in the oak-tree tops, soon began to warm her little, wet body. She got to her feet, she looked around. What a magical chorus of birds echoed all about her! They, at any rate, were happy, and friendly too. Blackbirds and thrushes came to inspect her, spotted henheads came cautiously from the fringe of the fern and made comforting chirruping sounds, erecting their queer spotted crests with excitement at seeing her, for of course she was the first human ever to penetrate thus far into the Forest.

Then she caught sight of a most curious little creature on a grassy bank on the other side of the stream. It appeared so comical she couldn't help smiling to herself, even though she was wet, cold, and hungry.

This creature was about the size of a fat squirrel. It appeared to have no arms and, indeed, no face, or – if it had a face – this was hidden under long hair. The head was very like a mop, the body round, not unlike a toy teddy bear's.

It was of course a cowzie, though little Helda didn't know that, for this was the first she had ever seen.

The little animal seemed to be quite unaware of her presence. It lay on its back, warming its small furry tummy in the rays of the sun which shone full and warm upon the bank, so that the bracken fronds were dry and did not glisten. It lay full length with its two powder-puff feet wide apart, revelling in the warmth as does a cat before a fire.

All at once the cowzie saw her and sat up. The change which came over it was most surprising. In a moment it had shrunk to half its size and appeared quite long and thin, the hair lying flat upon head and body.

If you have ever seen an old owl sitting in a tree half-asleep and unbothered by teasing birds, you will have noticed how round and fluffy it was. But at any alarm the owl shrinks to half its size, it elongates itself, it closes its dark, betraying eyes, until it appears like a sliver of worm-riddled wood.

It was just the same with the cowzie. From where Helda stood it appeared to have become nothing but a shrivelled frond of bracken. The camouflage was marvellous.

Now, thought little Helda, this little animal is frightened. It will presently run into the fern and I shall be alone. I shall starve. I shall never find my way out of this great Forest. O dear! whatever shall I do? How I wish I was back at home with my lovely grey geese and my dear father and mother! And the little girl buried her face in her hands and began to sob.

For some minutes the cowzie remained motionless, secretly regarding her, still pretending to be a frond of dead bracken. Then slowly its fur began to assume its former fluffy appearance. This was a sign that it was less frightened.

Timidly at first, then becoming more bold, it came down to the edge of the stream and without more ado came swimming across. It swam like a vole, indeed, it looked very like one in the water. Little Helda could see the air bubbles meshed in its fine fur, giving it a milky tinge.

It landed on a sunken log just below the sobbing girl and gave itself a vigorous shake which enveloped it in a misty cloud of spray. Then it advanced, still rather warily, until it was close to Helda.

All the time the little girl had been watching the cowzie through a crack in her fingers (which was rather deceitful of her, for she was crying and sobbing as though she was oblivious of anything else in the world but her woebegone state).

Obviously the cowzie was still unsure of its reception and just a little scared. Its fur kept going flat and then bushing out again; you could almost see it thinking, by watching the action of its fur. But the little goose-girl still held her head in her hands and

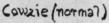

Cowzie (normal)   Cowzie (scared)

kept on sobbing, and the cowzie (they are gentle creatures and always anxious to please) began to speak to her. It spoke in a most curious bubbling way, very like the chatter of a budgerigar.

Of course, Helda couldn't understand a word, but it was obvious this little creature was trying to help her. She stopped crying. She then had the idea that if she showed, by signs, she was famished, the cowzie might be able to do something about it. So she rubbed her tummy and pointed at her mouth, and rubbed her tummy again. Then, it occurred to her, if I rub my tummy *too* much this little creature may think I've eaten something which has disagreed with me! So she tried another tack. 'Eat, eat, want something to EAT,' said Helda, pointing again to her mouth.

The cowzie made more extraordinary noises under its fur mask. Helda peered at it, trying to see what the face was like, if there really *was* a face, but the hair was so thick she couldn't see anything.

I'm not getting anywhere at all with this creature, said Helda to herself. If it comes any closer I'll try and grab it. I might even knock it on the head and eat it.

Luckily for Helda she did nothing of the sort which, anyway, would have been most ungrateful and cruel. And cowzies have teeth like razors and are immensely lithe and strong. She would certainly have been badly bitten had she tried any tricks like that. In any case, the cowzie, after bowing in a comical fashion four or five times in quick succession, turned round and swam back to the far bank. It turned round once to look at her and then the green fern swallowed it up.

'Oh dear!' cried Helda. 'Now I'm alone again! *What* a stupid little creature, I wish I'd caught it now.'

She sat on the grass staring across the stream at the thick Forest. The sun was very hot now. The leaves of the chestnuts and the oaks were without movement, layer upon layer, like green flounces to a petticoat, with cool mysterious shadows under each. Multitudes of insects of all kinds, some like brilliant blue and emerald and ruby jewels, passed back and forth in front of this screen of leaves, insects that Helda had never seen before.

There was a rustling in the fern on the other side of the stream. Something made Helda lie down out of sight. She was quite hidden by the fronds, which formed enclosing walls and ceiling, but she could peep out between the rough stems. She felt very alone, very lost, very afraid.

The ferns shook a little. A lower branch of briar, upon which grew the first of the dog-roses, sprang back as though released from a weight.

In an opening in the underwood was framed a huge savage face. Set in it were two glittering eerie eyes, and pale tusks curled up on either side of a black and brutish snout. Two hairy ears were cocked forward. The creature appeared to be staring straight at Helda. But it wasn't really, it was only making a cautious survey of the land.

Helda now knew what it was – one of the great striped Forest of Boland boars. She had sometimes seen them on late summer evenings when herding her geese back from the edge of the Forest. Usually they were shy, for they had learnt to fear the spears and arrows of the peasants in the villages. But this one might never have seen a human. Helda thought it best to lie low – a wise decision.

The huge, rough, weird-looking creature came out of the fern, snorting and stamping one forefoot. The flies were annoying him; they buzzed in a black halo around his floppy ears and he kept on ducking and tossing his great savage head.

Helda watched him trot down to the edge of the stream and drink. Apparently he was very thirsty for he drank and drank. Then, with a short half-squeal, half-grunt, he wheeled about, stood for a moment staring at the wall of sunlit leaves, with the water dropping like pearls from his brutish tusks, and lumbered off. Then there was nothing but the hum of the flies again. This hum grew in volume as the sun gained power, louder, louder.

Gorgeous butterflies appeared. They were so lovely that even Helda, hungry and anxious as she was, couldn't help catching her breath. There was one which came floating over the dog-roses that seemed as big as a bird. It glided and floated about, settling now and again upon the lower leaves, a shimmering blaze of brilliant azure blue.

Sometimes when the sun went behind a cloud for a moment and a shadow passed over the forest, it closed its wings. Then it was hard to pick it out from the leaf on which it sat, save for one vivid blue and deep-crimson eye which seemed to be looking at Helda all the time.

I don't know how long she lay there, becoming more hungry every minute, but at last the fern shook again and out popped a cowzie, followed by another, and another, until they came crowding out of the green underwood in hundreds. Helda gasped. Down the bank they came and over the stream.

Helda looked right and left and as far as she could see on either hand the sluggish water was furrowed and arrow-headed by the wakes of swimming cowzies, and each one shook itself like a dog when it came to land. Some carried in their teeth huge leaves sewed up with some sort of creeper, and two cowzies together seemed to be carrying between them a little woven basket made of willow.

They flowed about Helda in a bobbing mass. The basket was put down in front of her and the bearers stood back on either side and with a deft movement of their teeth they removed the large dock leaves which were covering the contents.

Inside the basket Helda saw four gleaming trout – each half a pound in weight. They were raw, for cowzies do not cook their food like the gnomes and humans do. But raw fish is very good to eat, as the Japanese well know. Helda picked one up by the tail and head and holding it cross-wise, like an otter, she bit into the back. It was quite delicious.

As she ate, the cowzies formed a furry wall about her, bobbing and shifting and all murmuring together, staring and jostling. Helda noticed their curious smell – not at all unpleasant; a sort of cosy smell, like a basket full of chickens.

She soon polished off the fish, and at once other cowzies appeared in front of her with offerings wrapped in dock leaves: wafer-thin slices from the breasts of henheads – raw, of course, but Helda was still so hungry she gobbled them up; and, most delicous of all, three spotted new-laid henhead eggs, again quite raw, but very palatable.

Soon she could eat no more. She thanked the cowzies as best she could, gingerly stroking their heads and scratching their backs. They seemed to enjoy this and made quaint whirring sounds rather like the purring of cats, turning their comical heads completely round, like owls.

As she tickled them she looked very hard to see if they had any eyes. Now and again she actually managed to catch a glimpse of them under the long, hanging fur; intelligent sharp little eyes they were, as sharp as those of birds. Several cowzies seemed to smile with satisfaction as she stroked them and then she glimpsed their thin ivory teeth, as sharp as needles. Even their little wet black noses were visible at times; more snouts than noses perhaps, like those of hedgehogs.

After her meal, and the restless, anxious night before, Helda began to feel sleepy. She lay down in the fern and closed her eyes. She felt safe among her new-found friends. Now and again she half-lifted her eyelids and saw with some amusement the round heads of the cowzies shuffling in front of her and peering closely at her, lost in amazement. They were evidently intensely curious at this stranger in their forest, and no wonder.

Helda's thoughts began to get muddled. She heard the occasional shuffling in the ferns, and muted squeaks as one cowzie pushed another or trod on its toes. In the background, too, was the gentle talk of the stream as it glistened in the hot sunlight, and the faint singing of birds. Then she fell asleep.

It was late afternoon when Helda awoke. There

was a curious, thin, keening noise which was part of her dreams; then it became reality. She opened her eyes quietly, as one does after a refreshing sleep. The thin, high, keening sound, more like a mew, sounded from high above. She looked upwards at the cloudless summer sky which was of a beautiful deep Atlantic blue, and there, high above, wheeling round and round, was a spotted henhead hawk. The light shone through its spread pinions, and its barred tail was like a gorgeous fan. In measured, slow circles it drifted sideways and was lost at last behind the tops of the Forest trees.

Helda sat up and looked about her in alarm. The cowzies had gone. Only the trampled fern showed where they had been, only a few fish bones remained. She felt again the old sense of being alone; lost.

There was the friendly stream still babbling to itself, and this gave her comfort. But it seemed so engrossed in its own business, in its own journey, that she felt all the more solitary. Evidently the cowzies, having brought her food and inspected her to see if she was harmless, had gone off on their own affairs. 'At any rate,' said Helda to herself, 'it's no good just lying here hoping they will come back.'

She got to her feet, glancing down at her legs and toes. As I have said, Helda never wore shoes or boots, and she could walk over hard stones without discomfort. But the briars had scratched her brown legs, so she bathed them in the cool stream. The scratches smarted at first, then she could feel them no longer.

The goose-girl came out of the water and began to follow the bank of the brook, along its every twist and wind. Sometimes it looped right back on itself, but always it hurried on, with here and there a little waterfall, here a swift run over spotted shingle, and at the bends a deepish, tawny pool.

Helda was expert at tickling fish, for she often caught the spotted trout in this same brook outside the Forest. But she saw no sign of trout here, save an occasional dimple at the throat of a pool which might have been a small fish rising.

She hadn't been walking for more than a few minutes when she began to hear curious sounds. They came from ahead of her, down the course of the stream. Tappings, knockings, the unmistakable 'clap clap' of an axe on wood. Occasionally, too, high-pitched voices, like the jabberings of wild geese. But all these sounds were very *small* sounds, like the tappings of woodpeckers, and the babblings of birds.

Helda was at once hopeful, yet she was afraid. She thought of all the things she had heard about the Forest of Boland, about its fairy folk, dwarfs, hobbits, elves, and so forth. Were those tales really true, she wondered?

She walked as quietly as she could through the bracken until a bend of the stream revealed a most amazing sight. She was so overcome she sank down among the fern.

About fifty yards away swarms of little men were busy over the remains of a diminutive trestle bridge which had evidently suffered considerable damage in the recent floods.

They were squat little creatures with huge hairy ears and big noses. Some wore beards, others were without any hair on their little berry-red faces. They wore hats of wonderful variety; some mere skull caps, or leather berets, others quite ornate with feathers in them and with wide brims. Their little coats were of leather, so were their breeches. Those working on the bank wore hide boots and leggings, but those in the stream were bare legged. All had very large feet and hands, and not one of them stood higher than Helda's knees.

There was one gnome who stood apart. He was dressed in a sort of blue uniform with a helmet. He twirled a truncheon in one hand and seemed to be a very important person indeed; a policeman, as we know. Several gnomes had placed their little ladders in the stream and were busy over the upper part of the bridge. A little to the right, close to the bole of a huge beech tree, there was a little sentry-box, and propped up against it, chewing a grass stem, was another gnome, obviously a guard. He had a wooden helmet, a metal breastplate, a circular shield, and metal plates on his shins such as you see in pictures of Roman centurions in your history books. She noticed that a business-like dagger was stuck in his leather belt and a small cross-bow couched in the crook of his arm. Now and again he'd take a careful look around, and once he seemed to be staring straight at Helda as she lay in the fern.

Now, from what the goose-girl had heard from her father about these Little People of the Forest, they were best left alone. It's quite true that nobody in the village had ever harmed or caught one of these Little People, but from time to time they *had* been seen (or people had thought they had seen them) whilst gathering wood on the fringes of the Forest in autumn.

She remembered, too, now she came to think of it, that only last year a swine-herd from the village, Wogan, whilst rounding up the village pigs – which were foraging for acorns – had gone too far into the Forest and had fallen into a deep pit which had been dug in a narrow riding. This pit had been cleverly concealed with branches so that he was into it before he knew what was happening. It wasn't very deep, Wogan said, he'd managed to scramble out again. But as he ran back down the path *someone had shot an arrow at him* and it had stuck in his leather breeches (and a little deeper, be it said).

Wogan brought the arrow back to the village to show that he was not making up a tale, and on Wizard Homm's advice it had been publicly burnt. The wound made by that arrow was nearly the end of him. He couldn't sit down for six months afterwards. (No doubt, as Helda's father said, the arrow, which was about nine inches long, had been dipped in some sort of poison.)

No, thought the goose-girl, I won't be like Wogan, I won't have anything to do with these little people They might shoot me full of those horrid arrows.

Yet the sight of real live gnomes busy at their work was so fascinating that Helda just couldn't help staying where she was and studying them. I'm sure I should have done the same.

They were as busy as beavers. Some were lashing the tops of the trestle poles together, others were hammering in nails with little wooden mallets; and from the Forest on either hand Helda could hear the sounds of continual chopping as more sapling trees were felled to repair the damage of the floods.

Then the fat gnome who appeared to be a policeman blew a long shrill blast on a wooden whistle. From somewhere among the trees a horn answered loud, quavering, and clear, and at once the gnomes began to put on their coats and to knock off work for the day.

They gathered in groups on either bank. Some pulled out pipes from their pockets and began to smoke, and all chattered away as merry as a bunch of starlings.

From far away another whistle sounded and soon a 'chuff-chuffing' noise. It sounded to Helda as though some large animal were panting in distress. Puh! Puh! Puh! Puh! The sounds drew closer, echoing back from the close-crowding trees, and the next moment Helda saw three little trucks moving out from behind the ferns. They were pushed by a small green engine with a bright copper dome and a tall funnel. Of course, Helda had never even heard of such a thing as an engine, but she could see at once it was some sort of vehicle on wheels. The smoke puffed from the long funnel and in the cab two gnomes were leaning out, peering back down the line, shouting and waving their hands.

With a faint banging of buffers, and many shouts and toots of horns and whistles, the train came to a stop a few feet from the bridge. Then there was a scramble as the gnomes piled into the trucks; some even hung on to the engine tender or climbed up upon the stacked wood which was stored there.

After a lot more shouting and running to and fro, and much striding up and down on the part of the policeman, all were aboard at last. With many wavings to the guard by the bridge the train gathered speed and disappeared among the trees. For a long time Helda could hear the faint puffing of the engine and, once, a faint long whistle. The guard after a long cautious look round, retired into his sentry-box.

Helda listened to the faint 'phut-phutting' of the engine dying away into the distance, and then all she could hear was the sound made by the stream gurgling round the piles of the trestle bridge fifty yards away. She decided there and then that nothing would induce her to go near the bridge or the sentry whose arrows were, no doubt, just as painful as the one which Wogan brought back from the Forest. These little men didn't seem attractive, like the cowzies. How she wished the cowzies would come back and bring her some supper, for Helda was a growing girl and the exercise and excitement had made her hungry again, *very* hungry.

Carefully, so as not to step on any twig or rustle the green bracken, Helda got to her feet, and bending as low as she could she retraced her steps along the side of the stream the way she had come.

But she had not reckoned with the extremely acute hearing of the sentry by the big beech tree. You see, the gnomes of the Forest of Boland were all possessed of good hearing but the regular guards had better hearing than any, and were specially chosen.

I don't suppose she'd gone more than five yards before something went past her with a *surrush*! and a *thuck*! and there, with its black-and-white feathered head still quivering among the fern, was an arrow just like the one that Wogan had brought home in the back of his leather pants!

Helda was a girl with plenty of presence of mind. In those days you had to have your wits about you, even when you were ten years old (which was Helda's age), if you wanted to survive at all.

She never turned round to see who had fired the arrow. She knew that in another moment a second one would be coming. She whipped aside into the fern. As she did so there was another *surrush*! and a louder *thuck*! and there was another arrow, shivering in a birch tree just behind her head.

Helda was terrified; she ran and ran. She stumbled and regained her feet, the brambles clawed at her, they ripped her already tattered dress, they cut her poor brown legs still further, and these were soon covered from the knees downwards in weals from thorns and whitish nettle stings.

But still she ran and ran. . . . Suddenly the trees and thick bushes parted and she fell forwards into a small open place where soft grass grew. As she lay gasping, three cats which had been playing on the little open lawn-like enclosure in front, raced spitting and with bottle-brush tails up the nearest beech bole.

Now, even though little Helda was so exhausted, frightened, and near to tears, the sight of those three cats astonished her very much. She thought at first they must be wild ones, but after hanging spread-eagled on the smooth bark of the beech and staring at Helda out of their wide-open green eyes, they dropped to the grass and ran towards her in quite a friendly way, lifting their tails, whirring and purring, and brushing their soft bodies against her poor torn legs.

They seemed quite delighted to greet her. Helda hadn't seen a cat since she left the village. How these three had appeared in the very heart of the Forest of Boland was quite beyond her!

Back and forth they primly tiptoed, with tails straight up, purring with evident delight. Helda would have liked to stay and play with them but she hadn't forgotten the deadly arrows. Perhaps the gnomes were already behind her in the fern, fitting more to their bow-strings. She got to her feet, and at once the cats ran off in front of her, scampering along in a most playful manner as though to show her the way. Helda followed as fast as she could.

Perhaps these cats belonged to a human, perhaps to

a woodcutter or a charcoal-burner. Even though she had been told, again and again, that nobody lived in the Forest of Boland save creatures which would do one harm, there *was* a chance that the villagers were wrong; after all nobody had ever dared to go into the Forest so how could they know what they were talking about?

The cats led her across the little clearing towards some big dark rocks. The nearer Helda drew to these rocks the slower was her step. At last she stopped behind a tree and peeped round cautiously. This is what she saw.

The rocks, which were hung with ivy and green with hart's-tongue fern, rose in a jumbled wall in front of her. Close to the twisted stem of a red-barked yew, whose thick green boughs spread like an umbrella overhead, she saw the mouth of a dark cave. Sitting in front of the cave, on a tree stump, was a figure which was at once familiar. It was that of an old man with a long white beard. On his head was a black cylindrical hat, and he wore a tattered blue robe. In front of him a huge leather-bound book was resting on his knees! He had large horn-rimmed glasses on his snipey nose and he was mumbling to himself as he studied the big book! And beside him, on the grass, were a small bottle, half full of blue liquid, bunches of herbs, and a collection of small white bones and skulls.

IT WAS WIZARD HOMM!

Helda's first impulse was to run to him and throw

her arms round him, for even a Wizard is less fearful than little squat men who shoot at you with poisoned arrows. But Helda was a cautious girl. The situation was a somewhat delicate one. She knew perfectly well she had cheeked Wizard Homm that time in the village, and she knew he'd looked very cross. Still, he'd probably forgotten all about the incident. But what on earth was he doing here, right in the heart of the Forest? That was indeed a puzzle!

The cats scuttled round him in circles. One jumped on his shoulder and nearly knocked off his tall hat, but the Wizard took no notice. He was deeply engrossed in making a spell, and by the look of things he was making quite a good one, for as Helda watched the form of the Wizard seemed to grow all misty. It was wavering like a reflection in water or the picture in your television set when it needs adjusting. She wasn't sure whether it was her own eyesight which was at fault or whether the Wizard really was vanishing.

Soon the only thing she could see clearly was the big book. This still remained apparently suspended in mid air, its leaves flat open, and faintly stirring in the wind; and the cat was still sitting there, up in the air where the Wizard's shoulder had been.

The next moment the form of the Wizard grew solid again and there he was, just as she had first seen him, with his long nose buried in his book. But now he was smiling to himself. She could hear him muttering, and once he laughed, a low dry cackle of glee.

Now I must admit that Helda had always taken the Wizard with a pinch of salt, as the saying is. She had only half-believed in Wizards anyway. But now, here indeed was proof that this one could work magic, and work it very well!

I think the little goose-girl would have done better to have made friends with the gnomes than with Wizard Homm. When she saw him disappear again, *twice* within the next five minutes I think she began to think so too. But unfortunately the Wizard decided it was time for something to eat. Having reappeared for the fourth time, he grabbed the cat on his shoulder which at once began to bite and scratch. Ignoring its struggles, for he held it firmly in his bony fingers, he pulled a whisker from its round snarling face.

Then he picked up some elder flowers from a bundle on the grass beside him, and very soon was busy with another spell. He had his back to Helda so she couldn't quite see what he was doing. But the next instant she saw him lean back on his improvised stool and smile to himself with an air of great satisfaction.

He corked up the little bottle carefully, which contained the mysterious bright blue liquid, and put it in the pocket of his gown. And even as Helda watched, a misty cloud formed in the air in front of him. Soon her eyes were popping out of their sockets for something solid was forming in the centre of the misty cloud. It was a small wooden table, a table spread with a snowy-white cloth. On that cloth were

savoury dishes from which very soon began to waft the most mouth-tickling odours to the small, uptilted, pretty nose of the starving goose-girl.

Soon, there it was, solid and real, *a lovely big steak-and-kidney pie*, with knobbly brown crust and battlemented edges, which emitted jets of savoury steam as the Wizard cut into it. From another dish (which had taken just a second or two longer to materialize) Helda saw the Wizard spoon out a few potatoes speckled with chopped mint, and from yet another dish he ladled tender young carrots!

O dear! dear! dear! *poor* little hungry Helda! How could she have lain there in the Forest alone and starving and endured those sights and smells? Now she knew Wizard Homm really *was* a Wizard, perhaps he'd be able to show her the way home again to her beloved parents, and all the old, dear, sights and sounds that her heart ached for: the familiar thatched wooden huts, the smell of wood-smoke, the lowing of the big heavy ploughing oxen her father used in the fields, and the musical cranking and wild cries of her portly ganders when she herded them home in the still summer evenings – what would she not give to see and hear these things once more! Anyway, he would surely give her a generous helping of that glorious pie!

Yet for some moments Helda battled with her wiser impulses which told her to have nothing to do with the Wizard.

Alas! It was some hours since her last meal. If she chose to turn away, how could she ever get another? Her friends the cowzies seemed to have forsaken her, and the gnomes were definitely hostile. She decided to make herself known to him. Quietly she stepped out from the fringe of the Forest, quietly and timidly she approached over the green grass.

Wizard Homm at that moment was just raising a forkful of steak-and-kidney pie towards his gravy-stained beard. For a second he seemed absolutely aghast, as though he could not believe his eyes. He was frozen with horror and astonishment, and the rich brown gravy drip-dripped from his fork to his plate.

'Please, mighty Wizard Homm, it's me, little Helda, the goose-girl from the village below your cave! Please, sir! I'm lost, sir! I was swept into the forest on father's pig trough in the big storm and I've been wandering ever since and . . . and . . . *please*, Wizard Homm, give me something to eat! I'm starving, Wizard Homm! . . . *please*, PLEASE help me!'

The Wizard slowly put down his knife and fork and nervously wiped his mouth with the tip of his beard. For some moments he was unable to speak. All sorts of ideas were rushing through his mind. Perhaps Helda's father was hiding close by – ready to dash out and club him – perhaps this was a trap of some sort.

The Wizard's sharp eyes flickered round, examining the background of the Forest – the thick bushes, the dark trees. But all seemed peaceful, birds sang and midges danced. At last he found his voice:

'Umm! Humm! Hurrum! So *you're* little Helda, are you?' He adjusted his big glasses and looked at her over the rims with rather a grim expression. 'Yes, yes, to be sure, now I see you are – I remember you well. Are you not that cheeky little girl who was so rude to me and my cats down in the village?'

Helda's head hung down, her cheeks went crimson. She did not answer. Tears welled up; they filled her big blue-green eyes, trickled down her grimy little face and splashed warm upon her bare scarred toes.

'Umm,' said Wizard Homm again, looking at her severely over his glasses, 'little girls who cheek Wizards sometimes find that it doesn't pay. Where's your father, goose-girl?'

'I – I – I – do – n-n-not know, mighty Wizard! He may have been drowned in the great flood. How should I know where he is?' She threw herself on the grass and her shoulders shook and shook. She sobbed bitterly.

Now, if Wizard Homm had been a nice kind old Wizard (and some Wizards *were* kind in those far-off days), he might have forgiven little Helda for being rude to him; he might have taken pity on such a pretty little girl who was lost and distressed.

But he was not of a forgiving nature and, as we know, he was a sneaky, rather nasty old Wizard, who would have liked to turn you into a caterpillar or a sheep-tick as soon as look at you, if it benefited him at all.

Moreover, he hadn't forgotten how Helda's father

had set the villagers against him and driven him from the cave where he had lived for years past counting. He wasn't in the least sorry for the goose-girl. He was already thinking of all sorts of ways of punishing her. After all, he thought to himself with a sort of pride, it's because I put a spell on her she is here at all. She would be just the thing he wanted for his experiments with spells and he'd turn her into something really nasty.

Wizard Homm felt he was going to enjoy himself. When next he spoke he didn't appear angry any more; indeed, his cracked old voice was quite whiny and wheedly.

'Stop crying, my little goose-girl, stop crying, that won't do you any good. Come, sit at my table, and have some of this excellent steak-and-kidney pie! I can recommend it. And if you would like some orange juice, or grapefruit, or better still, stone ginger (all little girls like that), pray say so. I can recommend this red wine – Beaune, best vintage – but that would no doubt be too heavy for your infant taste.'

Helda raised her tear-stained face. The Wizard was actually smiling, but it was really rather a dreadful smile. The thin pale mouth, half-hidden in gravy-stained whiskers, was certainly smiling, his cheeks were creased with smile-lines, but when little Helda looked at the Wizard's eyes, they weren't smiling at all. They seemed to belong to a different face altogether.

Nevertheless, though something told little Helda to turn and run, the smell of the pie, the sight of its shiny brown crust, the rich thick gravy, the smooth, pale as ivory, infant potatoes, the tender, orange-coloured carrots reposing in their respective white dishes, were too much for her. Slowly she came to the table and stood with hanging head, looking at the Wizard from under her thick black lashes.

'Sit down, child, sit down and stop hiccupping,' said the Wizard again, 'make yourself at home. You must indeed be hungry after your adventures in flood and forest! Have some pie.'

Helda looked vaguely round for something to sit on. To her surprise, she found, just behind her, a curious chair which certainly hadn't been there a moment before. This was of what we should call modern design, the very latest pattern such as you and I can see in any large store today; an affair of tubular steel and canvas.

Cautiously she sat down on it. It was certainly quite comfortable, though it looked so odd and didn't match the table at all.

The steak-and-kidney pie, to say nothing of the new potatoes with little green bits of mint on them, and the tender carrots, *and* the gravy, were very, *very*, good indeed, much better than anything she'd ever tasted in her life before. Better than pig's trotters, of which she was so fond at home, better than roast goose even; certainly it was better than the raw trout which the cowzies had brought her.

Helda ate, and ate, and ate. She forgot the Wizard, she forgot everything but the heaped plate before

her and that scrumptious steak-and-kidney pie!

She ate so ravenously she never noticed that the
Wizard was slipping something into the tall glass
of stone ginger beside her plate. When at last she
paused from eating, she grasped the glass and drank
and drank. And all the time the Wizard sat and
watched, his mouth and cheeks smiling, but the
eyes belonging to somebody else.

She drained the glass and asked for more. The
Wizard obligingly poured her out another. And
then – things went all thick and far away.

The background of forest trees was no longer fixed
and steady but actually waving like a curtain stirred
by a gentle breeze. She seemed to see the Wizard rise
from his seat and begin a slow dance. He was holding
up his blue gown in his right hand and with the
other he was pointing at her with a crooked, skinny
finger. On each shoulder sat a cat, the third was
crouched on top of the tall black hat. And as the
Wizard danced he began to sing in a cracked skinny
voice:

> 'Helda Halberd shall be mine,
> I've put snoreweed in her wine.
> Never more shall she go free,
> Henceforth she belongs to me!'

The Wizard began to spin round and round until
he was the shape of a misty dumb-bell, and poor
Helda held her head in both hands. She couldn't take

her eyes off the spinning shape before her. The cracked voice seemed to be coming to her down a long, long, tunnel, and it was chanting more slowly now as he pronounced a spell:

> 'Snoreweed, snoreweed, lovely brew,
> Yew-dark magic conjure you,
> Till your earth-enchanted deep
> Draws your eyelids down in sleep.
> Snoreweed, snoreweed, simmer there,
> Twilight trembles in the air,
> Darkness drawn from unknown deep
> Lose your cares in faëry sleep.
> Far from realms of mortal men
> Till I wish you light again.'

Dimly Helda was aware that the table and the remains of the supper had somehow vanished. Gradually the Wizard was ceasing to revolve, indeed he was wobbling on his legs now, just like a spent spinning-top, and the black hat was leaning outwards and wobbling too! Hat and shoulders spilled the cats off sideways and then . . . all that remained on the green grass in front of the cave was a little girl fast asleep and the wicked Wizard and his three cats looking at her!

7

THE BOOK OF SPELLS

WHEN Helda woke up she found it was morning. She was lying on the grass in front of the Wizard's cave. She had a splitting headache (the result of the snoreweed, of course). There was something heavy round her ankle, something very hard. She put down her hand and felt it. She found it was an iron collar. Attached to the collar was a chain, which was fastened securely to a post driven into the ground. Though her hands were free and she could walk about, she was tethered very securely, just as if she were one of her father's cows, which were always tethered in this way in case they wandered away into the Forest.

I think you can imagine that this discovery of Helda's was not a pleasant one. It isn't very comfortable to be wearing a heavy iron collar round your ankle, and it's still more uncomfortable to walk about with one attached to a long chain.

There was no trace of the Wizard. The only sign of life was a trembling in the oak leaves near by where Ding, Dong, and Belle were playing about like squirrels. Now and again little bits of bark and bruised leaves fell on to the grass under the tree as

the cats ran up and down and wrestled with each
other among the oak boughs. Any other time they
would have been pretty to watch, but Helda dis-
trusted the cats now, for it was they who had led to
her capture by Wizard Homm.

Poor Helda got to her feet, rather unsteadily, and
the chain made a clanking noise. The rustling in the
oak leaves stopped at once. For Ding, Dong, and

109

Belle were looking at her through the chinks in the leaves. Their three round faces were all in a line and they watched her as intently as if she were a mouse.

Helda picked up the links of the chain and felt the fastening where it joined the collar. The last link seemed to be riveted to the collar ring. No chance of unfastening that!

Dragging the chain Helda walked across to the post. That was just as secure. She tried to shake it but it wouldn't budge. All the time the cats watched her.

Helda was muddled by the snoreweed. She tried to remember what had happened. She could remember finding the cats and the very good supper the Wizard gave her, and how hungry she had been. That was all. It was quite certain the Wizard had made her his prisoner and he'd probably something unpleasant in store for her.

Poor Helda sat down with her arms round the big wooden post. She began to cry bitterly. The tears ran down her cheeks, they splashed warm on her bare knees. She was hungry again too, which made matters worse, and the iron collar was making her little ankle very sore.

Ding, Dong, and Belle having run up the oak were now trying to get down. Cats are silly about climbing trees. They can go up quickly enough but it's a different matter coming down, as many have found when climbing a cliff.

First they tried to come down head first, but they felt their claws slipping. Then they turned round and tried to come down backwards, but they couldn't see where they were going, so they went up again spitting and swearing. Then they began to mew plaintively. They wanted Wizard Homm to come back and help them down.

Meanwhile little Helda stopped crying. She had been crying because she was sorry for herself, which is one of the chief reasons why children cry. She was thinking what a pathetic picture she made, chained to a post with her shoulders shaking and the big hot tears splashing on her bare knees. And as there was nobody to be sorry for her, and the cats didn't seem in the least interested, she dried her eyes with the back of her hands.

Perhaps the Wizard was looking at her from the shadows of the cave! She saw the long ivy creepers hanging down against the gloom beyond, but there wasn't a sound in there. All round the cave were huge mossy rocks the size of small houses. Some were sprouting trees, dark yew trees which seemed to spring right out of the centres of the blocks of stone. There was no sound but the thin mewing of the cats, a maddening noise.

What a chance to escape, now the Wizard was elsewhere! But she knew she could never undo the iron collar, so there was nothing to do but wait for her captor to return.

Then Helda noticed that just outside the cave was a very modern canvas chair. It was twentieth-century, in actual fact; what we know very well as a 'deck-chair'. It looked quite out of place in a forest glade, and of course Helda had never seen such a strange chair in her life. And beside it, on the grass, was an enormous leather-bound book, a stone bottle of what looked like ink, and a feather pen.

As we know, Helda could read quite well, which was really most unusual in a girl from such a humble home. So you can see what a lucky thing this was for her. If she hadn't been able to read, I don't know what would have been the end of her, I'm sure, so it does show that lessons come in useful sometimes.

When Helda tried to reach the book she found the chain wasn't quite long enough but she was a resourceful girl. She lay down flat on her tummy. She found she could just touch the book with the tips of her fingers, though it wasn't easy to drag it towards her. But inch by inch she managed it.

She read the title (in Latin, of course, which I won't bother you with) – *Wizard Wizardry*. And then, opening the book, she was soon quite absorbed. It really *was* a most fascinating book. There were lots of funny little drawings in brown ink, some looking as if they had been drawn in blood, long, long ago.

Here and there Wizard Homm had added a few marginal notes of his own, such as 'might try this', 'utter bunkum', 'quite efficacious' – which was such a long word that Helda didn't understand it at all, nor do you.

It dawned on Helda that if she could only work one of these spells she might get the 'whip hand', as the saying is, of Wizard Homm. The idea came to her quite suddenly. But then she thought that, after all, no spells would be any good to anyone who wasn't a Wizard. In this, however, she was quite mistaken, as we shall see all in good time. Slowly she turned the heavy pages which were made of parchment and smelt like old boots.

'I wonder,' said Helda to herself, 'I wonder if there's anything about breaking chains?'

She looked under C.

'Cat's-whiskers, Chilblains, Cold in the head, no – nothing there.'

Then she looked under F.

'Fats, Frogs, Fleas, *Fetters.* Ah! what about this!

'*FETTERS. How to be free from. Take three seeds of Moonwort, swallow them whole, and recite:*

> *Locks I break,*
> *Nails I draw,*
> *Fetters cast,*
> *For evermore.*
> *Horse go lame,*
> *Feet go sore,*
> *Moonwort magic,*
> *Certain, sure!'*

Helda said the magic words to herself over and over again. They had a certain lilt about them, they stuck in her mind. If only she had some moonwort seed! At the back of this massive tome were drawings of all the herbs and plants mentioned in the spells, quite ten pages of drawings, all very cleverly done by the Wizard himself in the long winter evenings, and all duly signed neatly at each page corner, with the date.

There were drawings of dandelions (and of course snoreweeds), of pickpockets and pimpernels, of pennyworts and prunellas. And of course there were a lot of plants that we don't know of, which grew long, long ago in the Forest of Boland. But they were all there, every one.

'Really,' said Helda to herself, as she turned the pages, 'they are most beautifully drawn! I should never have believed it! But then, he's a Wizard, and I suppose Wizards can do most things.'

She turned to the Ms.

Under M she found quite a list of plants, flowers, grasses, and ferns, all neatly drawn (with marginal notes by the Wizard).

Meliot, Moschatel, Maidenhair, Marshweed, Merlin's Grass, Miltwaste, MOONWORT, ah! here it was, and a drawing, too, beside it, with notes by the Wizard. *Moonwort. Heathy parts of Boland Forest under elders and yews. Might come in useful for cracking open chests. Good for hammer-toes.*

Helda had become so interested in the book of spells that she had quite forgotten where she was. She had even forgotten she still had a collar round her ankle, and that she was chained like a gipsy's horse to a picket. She was brought back to reality with a jump.

Something thumped on to the grass beside her. There was a scuffling and a spitting. Helda turned round just in time to see Belle fall out of the oak tree. The cat landed on her feet, as all cats do, and all three made off into the ferns as fast as they could go with their tails straight up in the air.

Now Helda wasn't at all sure if the cats could speak. Being Wizard's cats it was quite on the cards they did, and if so, they had certainly run off to tell the Wizard what his prisoner was up to.

She shut the big book at once, and lying down once again she pushed it away from her towards the deck-chair. This wasn't nearly so easy as pulling it towards her but somehow she managed to push it back, more or less into position. She had hardly done so when she heard footsteps shuffling through the underwood.

Wizard Homm came out of the shadows with his cats running behind him. He had a bag on his back full of herbs. He looked hot and tired. Helda, hunched up beside her post, appeared not to look at him. She buried her face in her hands and pretended to cry. But all the time she was peeping at the Wizard between her fingers to see what he was going to do.

8

A CHANCE OF ESCAPE

'Umph!' grunted the Wizard, slinging his bag of herbs off his back and dumping it under the oak tree.

'That's a good job done, to be sure. And how's my little Helda, my own little goose-girl, my fat pigeon? How do you like your nice bright chain?'

Helda didn't reply. She kept her fingers over her eyes, and continued to sniffle and snuffle.

'If you don't stop that noise I'll turn you into something I can put in a match-box,' snarled the Wizard, 'then I shan't have the trouble of keeping you chained up.'

Helda stopped snuffling at once, which was very wise of her. The Wizard might well carry out his threat. It would be awful to be turned into a wood-louse or a cockroach.

'Ah! that's better,' said the Wizard, 'and now, my pigeon, we'll have some lunch – that's if you're hungry. I've been tramping over half the Forest for plants. I'm ready for lunch if you aren't.'

'Can't I have this horrid chain off, please Wizard Homm?' asked Helda in a small meek voice. 'It's heavy and it's making my ankle sore!'

'Certainly not,' snapped the Wizard, 'what do you take me for goose-girl? You'd be off into the fern as quick as a rabbit and that's the last I should see of you. You'll get used to it, my fine fat pigeon, and it won't be for long, I daresay. Now for lunch!'

The Wizard picked up his book (Helda was relieved to see that he suspected nothing and evidently the cats hadn't 'sneaked' on her).

Soon the most delicious smells were making the air fragrant with mouth-tickling odours. A table of spotted bamboo gradually appeared, decked with a white cloth fringed with blue silk tassels. Then there materialized a bottle of Worcestershire Sauce (the authentic version, made from a recipe by a nobleman in that county).

This was quickly flanked by two plates of mock-turtle soup and half a cold pink salmon. The smell of this fish quickly brought Ding, Dong, and Belle from out of the ferns. They clustered about Wizard Homm, rubbing themselves against his shoes, purring and whirring and looking up and mewing so loudly that their round whiskered faces seemed to split in half like cut melons.

For sweet there were fresh strawberries and cream and fine white castor sugar. Poor Helda even forgot her chain, which made such a horrid clanking noise every time she moved. One thing was certain, Helda thought, whatever the Wizard intended to do with her, he certainly fed her well. Perhaps he was fattening her up, like a prize goose!

When luncheon was over, the table and all its contents gradually melted into thin air. Only Ding, Dong, and Belle, busy under the table with the backbone of the salmon, showed that everyone had really dined. The Wizard took off his shoes and stretched himself out on the soft grass in the shade of the oak. He was soon fast asleep. Helda had to remain out in the sun, chained to her post.

The heat was fearful, she felt rather sick. Perhaps she'd eaten too many strawberries. She watched the blubottles buzzing in and out of the Wizard's shoes, and a large green dragonfly settled on his black hat. She found a little shade from the post but it was a very little, *narrow* shade.

The sound of the Wizard's snores was awful! They began as little tiny ones and worked up to a climax, ending in a shuddering snort. Then they began all over again.

Meanwhile the cats were busy playing with the Wizard's bag of herbs. Their antics were so funny that even Helda, hot and weary in her chains, had to laugh at them.

First Ding hid behind the bag and Dong and Belle pretended not to see him. Then they chased each other round and round the bag with lightning speed. Then Belle hid *inside* the bag. Then they *all* got inside it. The bag began to rear up and writhe about as if alive, and this really *was* funny!

The cats began to pull out the herbs all over the grass, batting them with their paws, turning head over heels. Helda could see that the Wizard had been busy. All manner of plants were strewn about, sinister orchid leaves blotched with purple splashes, carrot-like roots of hemlock and hedge parsley,

scarlet fungi spotted with white, and I know not what else.

Suddenly, Belle picked up a herb and rushed off with it, pursued by Ding. The chase was fast and furious, and once both cats jumped right over the Wizard as he lay asleep. Then they came tearing across to Helda. Belle ran up the post with the herb in her mouth. As she sat there Helda saw at once that it was a plant exactly like that she had seen in the big book, a plant of *moonwort*!

Now, if that wasn't a piece of luck! Somehow or other Helda determined to have that plant. She made friendly noises and brought her left hand slowly up behind Belle who was watching Ding crouched below. In a flash she grabbed the cat by the scruff of the neck. It let out a noise like a burst water-pipe. The plant dropped right into Helda's lap.

There was a swearing and a spitting. Helda let go of Belle who was down the post and over the grass like a flash of light with Ding and Dong hard on her heels. They jumped right on to the Wizard (whether by design or accident I do not know) and Wizard Homm woke up in a fury. He sat up, glaring about him, his tall black hat at a rakish angle, and numerous spiders, woodlice, and earwigs dropped rapidly from his beard like rats leaving a burning ship. He made a grab at Belle but she jumped over his head and went up into the oak, while the other two cats ran into the cave.

'Drat those cats,' he muttered. He stared suspiciously at Helda, who had her back to him and was taking no notice. Then with a grunt he turned over and went to sleep again. Helda dug a little hole in the turf at the foot of the post. She put the moonwort plant in the hole, and covered it up again. Perhaps the spell wouldn't work as she wasn't a Wizard, but it would be worth trying! But not now. For when she next looked at the Wizard he was lying on his side with his face towards her. His cylindrical black hat was cocked drunkenly over one eye and Helda wasn't quite sure if that eye was fully shut. It looked as though it was but when she examined it more closely she wasn't so certain.

9

THE SPELL WORKS

WHEN the sun at last slid round behind the oaks and a cool shade was cast upon the grass before the cave, the Wizard awoke with a terrific snort. First he stared at Helda to make sure she was still safe, then he reached for his shoes and put them on.

It was then that he noticed the herbs strewn all about the grass. He was furious. I think he half-suspected Helda had been tampering with his herb bag. Then he realized it must have been the cats.

He picked the plants up, one by one, cursing and muttering all the time, for of course they had been lying in the sun and many were like limp grey strings.

Then he set to work to make drawings of the best preserved of them in his big book. He put on his big glasses and with a quill pen, which he dipped into a stone bottle, he set to work. Some of the herbs had been so shrivelled in the sun that they were useless. Helda could see he was in an ugly temper.

In fact, he was in such a bad temper that Helda didn't have any supper, nor did the cats. But you may be sure the Wizard treated himself to a good meal, and by the delightful scents which came wafting across it would seem that he was having fish and chips.

Ding, Dong, and Belle kept well out of the way. They could smell the fish but they daren't come near the cave. Whenever one showed itself the Wizard threw something at it. As for Helda he ignored her entirely; she might have been a tethered goat for all he cared. She felt very hungry, very thirsty, and the big iron collar was making her poor little leg terribly red and sore.

When the Wizard had finished his supper he went back to his work. There was no sound but the scratching of his pen on the parchment. Now and then he'd look up and glower at Helda over the tops of his glasses and a very nasty smile played about his thin lips.

As a matter of fact Wizard Homm was thinking all the time what he was going to do with Helda. He had never before experimented with humans and he was determined to try out his skill.

He was trying to think up the most interesting spell he could, and there were other things, too, which occupied his mind. In the far recesses of the cave was another bag but it did not contain herbs. O dear me no! What do you think was in that bag? Why – gold of course! Great lumps of the shining stuff! A few days before the Wizard had discovered a wonderful cave full of gold. He'd come upon it quite by accident, in actual fact he had been led to it by a strange little trackway made of strips of metal fastened to wooden sleepers! It was of course the mine at Poolewe. Having never before seen railway lines the Wizard couldn't make head or tail of them but he had followed them up, winding this way and that through the bracken, until he had come on the dragon's cave, the gnomes' cave, and it hadn't taken him long to find what was inside!

There were very curious scratches on the floor of the cave like huge pad marks and the place smelt like seaweed which has lain a long time in the sun. The Wizard noticed other queer things in that cave, little lamps hanging from the ceiling, for instance, and tiny pick-axes and shovels lying about.

Wizard Homm hadn't tarried very long, you may be sure, but he remained long enough to collect for himself a sack of gold which was so heavy it had taken him all his time to get it back to his own cave. And now, as Wizard Homm sat in his deck-chair studying his big book of spells, he was planning and scheming for all he was worth.

He had enough gold in the cave behind him to make him rich for life. He'd even be richer than the great Lord Boland who lived in the castle at home outside the Forest! He wouldn't have to rely on the miserable bits of silver he had from the peasants. He could live like the mighty noble himself if he wished; in fact he had everything now a Wizard could desire, riches and above all power, power in his spells which could make him master of all! No wonder he felt pleased with himself!

Suddenly an idea struck him. He didn't know why

he hadn't thought of it before! Why – of course – he'd turn the goose-girl into a donkey! On the donkey's back he would pile his gold and so transport his booty out of this dark and tangled Forest to the outside world! A splendid idea! The very thing!

Once out of the Forest he would perhaps build himself a castle, a castle even larger and finer than that owned by the Lord of the Manor, and if he had any trouble from the latter he'd soon deal with *him*, even though he had three hundred men-at-arms to fight for him. Against the Wizard and his book of spells (and the Dragon's Blood) nobody could prevail.

The Wizard rubbed his hands in glee. He got up from his stool and came shuffling across to Helda who lay quite motionless beside the post. 'And how's my little fat pigeon?' he cooed, stroking his long and dirty beard.

Helda began to cry. 'O *please*, Wizard Homm, *please* take off this horrid chain, it's making my ankle so sore!'

'Don't worry, my little pigeon, you won't be wearing it much longer, you'll be having a nice leather bridle instead. Tomorrow I'm going to turn you into a donkey, a nice little furry donkey. And on your back I'm going to pile all my gold, and my big book of spells, and we're going out of this Forest for good and all. You didn't know I was rich, did you, goose-girl? You don't believe me? Then I'll show you, and you can see what you'll have to carry for me tomorrow.'

The Wizard shuffled into the cave and emerged

with a bag which was indeed so heavy he had to drag it along the ground behind him. He undid the mouth. He pulled out a nugget of gold the size of his own head.

'There, my fat pigeon, look at that gold, solid gold! There's a stream by the cave where I found this gold. That stream is the Boland Water, no other stream of such size flows through the Forest, of that I'm certain. We're going to follow that stream up, and it will guide us back home out of this Forest for good and all. And *when* we get home I shall sell you to your own father, for he will no doubt be glad of a nice useful little donkey and perhaps he'll behave a little better when he knows how powerful I am. Ah! Ha! ha!' laughed Wizard Homm, 'yes, yes indeed, that *will* be a great joke, to sell Master Halberd his own daughter in the guise of a donkey! Well, well, well, that's a lesson to all little girls who cheek Wizards.'

When Helda heard these nasty spiteful plans she was overcome with horror. She knew that if her one remaining hope, the moonwort charm, should fail, then indeed, she would be turned into a donkey. She'd have to eat grass instead of strawberries and cream. She'd think, feel, hear and smell like a donkey, and never be a little girl again. No wonder she cried!

But the Wizard did not heed her crying. He wrapped his blue gown about him and went back to his cave. The shadows of the Forest began to gather thickly.

Helda lay, trembling, chained to her post. Over and over again she recited the magic words to herself. How did they go?

> 'Locks I break,
> Nails I draw,
> Fetters cast
> For evermore!
> Horse go lame,
> Foot go sore,
> Moonwort magic,
> Certain, sure!'

She took a sidelong glance at the black mouth of the cave, with its trailing ivy creepers and the dark yews sprouting from the rocks. Then she very secretly uncovered the hole and made sure her precious root of moonwort was safe and sound. Being sheltered from the sun it was still green, though a little limp.

Somewhere a nightjar started to whirr like a spinning-wheel. It was beautifully cool now in the Forest after the great heat of the afternoon.

White moths appeared and began dancing up and down over the fern, and the sweet sickly scent of honeysuckle came wafting from the bushes. Inside the cave Helda could hear the Wizard moving about, preparing for sleep. He was indeed so tired he hadn't even bothered to put away his book of spells. It lay on the seat of the deck-chair which was now far out of Helda's reach.

When it got quite dusk the three cats came out of the fern. They came stealthily like little tigers and their tails twitched. They stared at Helda and their eyes glowed a dull pink fire. One by one they stole into the darkness of the cave.

Helda lay very still by the post, her eyes on the dark cave mouth. Perhaps the Wizard would remember he'd left his book of spells outside and come and fetch it, but he didn't.

The white canvas of the deck-chair glimmered faintly in the shadows, darker grew the massive oaks and the brooding yews. A little moving shadow detached itself from the ferns and came across the grass right by Helda. It was a hedgehog. It snuffled about in the grass where the Wizard had had supper and, no doubt, found some crumbs there, for it routed about for quite a long time before trundling off down a forest path.

Helda's fingers felt under the turf for the moon-wort. She pulled out the queer little fern. She crumbled into the palm of her hand three of the little brown capsules. She popped them into her mouth and swallowed them down with one big gulp! Then, sitting back on her heels, she recited the magic words:

> 'Locks I break,
> Nails I draw,
> Fetters cast,
> For evermore!
> Horse go lame,

Foot go sore,
Moonwort magic,
Certain, sure!'

Instantly Helda felt the iron band about her ankle burst asunder with a loud twang. She jumped to her feet. She was free! FREE!

10

A PRISONER AGAIN

HELDA'S first impulse on finding that she was no longer chained was to run off into the bushes. She was, however, a brave and sensible girl and had a wise little head on her shoulders. She knew well enough she was dealing with a Wizard, and a powerful one at that. And what, thought Helda, is there to stop his making a spell to bring me back again?

No, if she must make *quite* sure about making good her escape she had better steal his book of spells! It was, you remember, a very heavy book, and she could not possibly carry it far. She would have to find some place to hide it; she might even throw it into the Boland Water, which the Wizard had said was close by. Then the stream would carry it away and that would be an end of it.

If it hadn't been so dark Helda might have even tried her hand at making some spells on her own account, for the moonwort seed had worked perfectly as we have seen. It would have been fun, for instance, to turn the Wizard into a donkey, just to pay him out. But she couldn't think of such things now, not in the dark. The sooner she got rid of such a dangerous book the better for everybody. So very,

very, quietly she tiptoed towards the chair which she could see palely glimmering near the mouth of the cave.

Step by step Helda approached the book, all the time watching the cave mouth out of the corner of her eye.

Six points of light were shining there, close to the ground. These lights were the eyes of Ding, Dong, and Belle, who were watching her. What if the cats ran back into the cave and told the Wizard?

Helda felt herself trembling violently which was not surprising. She had never been so scared in her life before. She bent down, put her hands round the book, and lifted it from the chair. She looked once more at the dark cave mouth. The gleaming eyes of the cats had vanished, but what she saw made her gasp. The Wizard was standing there, silently watching her, in his black pot hat and long gown sprinkled with stars. His hands were behind his back. His eyes seemed to gleam as brightly as those of his cats.

Crash! went the heavy book to the ground. Helda had barely turned to run when, with one stride, the Wizard caught her by the shoulder with a bony claw.

'Not so fast, little pigeon, not so fast. Dear me! tut! tut! how the pigeon struggles! Stay quiet now, goose-girl,' and he gave her a shake with a grip like an iron vice. 'So you managed to slip your chain, did you? Dear me! That *was* very clever of you! But maybe my book of spells helped you. Eh? It was silly of me not to turn you into a donkey last night, that would have saved us all this bother, wouldn't it? And I might have had my beauty sleep which all Wizards need. Never mind, we'll waste no more time.'

Wizard Homm, still keeping a rigid grip on Helda with his left hand, seized his stick (on which were carved serpents entwined) in his right, and with it he drew a circle round her on the grass, turning her about with him. As the Wizard's stick touched the grass it left a ripple of dull glow-worm light. Faster and faster he seemed to go. Helda found herself spinning with him, and all the time Wizard Homm was singing in a see-saw sort of voice:

> *Magic circle ring you round,*
> *Hold you fast upon this ground,*
> *Hold you fast till spell be sure,*
> *Treble chance and family four.'*

Then Wizard Homm let go of Helda's arm and

without another word went back into his cave leaving her standing helpless there. He never even looked back.

Helda tried to move her feet. It was exactly as if they were set in lead, she couldn't move a muscle! It was a horrid feeling, as you can well imagine, just like a bad dream! She wanted to shout for help. She couldn't utter a sound. On the grass, where the Wizard had made his circle with his staff, there was a softly glowing ring of light all round her which seemed to dance like fire-flies.

Soon the Wizard emerged from the cave again carrying his bag of herbs and a large bundle of dry firewood. He set the bag down outside the circle and began to stack the wood methodically into a sort of tent or pyramid of sticks.

'Sorry to keep you waiting, fat pigeon, I won't be long. No, don't be afraid, I'm not going to roast you, if that's what you are thinking, though you certainly deserve it and you would be nice and tender. I'm only going to turn you into a quiet little donkey who would never *think* of running away from her master! For, you see, we've got a long march tomorrow, you and I; my bags of gold will weigh heavy, and so will the book. Heigh! Ho! Never mind, we'll manage it all right, my nice little donkey and I, so we will!' He went off chuckling quietly to himself to get some more wood.

The Wizard seemed to take a long time in making the fire to his satisfaction. The cats were very interested. They kept getting under his feet. Now and

if it was going to work, but he had the right stuff for the job: Dragon's Blood, you could do anything with Dragon's Blood, and anyway experiments were always fun!

When the fire had changed to a tall, still, pillar of flame which cast a bright light all around and made the trees look a brilliant fairy-like green, the Wizard drew up his deck-chair. Settling himself down comfortably in it, he put on his big spectacles and with his book of spells on his knees he opened it at page eighty-one.

'*How to turn a virgin into a donkey.*' (A virgin means a young girl.) '*Take a minim of Dragon's Blood, mix with it two whole stalks of Merlin's Grass,*' (here the Wizard nodded and smiled to himself and patted his bag), '*boil over a fire in a little water for two minutes. Anoint the virgin. Recite these words:*

> '*Donkey's ears and donkey's nose,*
> *Donkey's tail and donkey's toes,*
> *Donkey's eyes, and donkey's teeth,*
> *Boomps a Daisy underneath!*'

The Wizard looked at Helda over his glasses. 'A most charming spell, my little pigeon, and one that I never thought I should have the chance to perform! It should not take long, goose-girl, it says here "allow three minutes". A remarkably quick spell under the circumstances, and I believe practically painless. It also says in the footnote, my little pigeon (and this should interest you), that once changed you can't be changed back. That's of no matter, however, for, as you know, I intend to sell you to your father, if ever we get out of this plaguey Forest. And now, my pigeon, I will take a little refreshment and then we can get to work.'

The Wizard muttered something under his beard, made a pass or two, swallowed a small leaf of horehound, and then sat back in his chair twiddling his thumbs.

Between Helda and the tall flames a small bamboo table appeared. She saw its legs first, transparent, wavering, with the light shining through them. They grew darker, and finally quite black and rigid, silhouetted against the brilliance of the fire.

Upon the table appeared a soda siphon, a glass, and a bottle of *Highland Dew* Scotch Whisky. The Wizard poured himself out a glass at once and sipped it with evident satisfaction, tickling the round, soft heads of his purring cats with his free hand.

Poor Helda, helpless, and unable to move, could only stare at the high flames and think bitterly how near she had been to making her escape. If only she hadn't tried to steal the book! If only she had run off into the darkness and chanced whether the Wizard made a spell to bring her back! Too late now to think of these things!

She was sure that turning into a donkey was going to be an uncomfortable business, and, anyway, she had no desire to *be* a donkey, and I don't blame her, do you? If only her friends the cowzies, those

queer little fluffy creatures, were here to help her!
But alas, there were no cowzies within miles. The
only people that night who saw the glow from the

Wizard's fire were some gnome guards on night duty at Boland Water station, many leagues away across the Forest, and they thought it was a forest fire.

The Wizard finished his whisky, then he had a second glass which made him merry. His tall black hat was soon at quite a rakish angle and he was breathing heavily in his beard.

Helda watched the flames dancing behind the legs of the table. She watched the glow of light on the soda siphon, that strange magical bottle, with its upward-speeding pearls of bubbles, which made such a funny squirting sound (even the Wizard seemed a little timid when he pressed the trigger).

At last the table blurred and melted. Then there was only the naked fire, dancing and leaping. Wizard Homm was peering and muttering, the firelight glinting on his glasses, his dirty claw tracing the lines of print on the page.

He shut the book, put it down on the grass, and got up from his chair. Then he rolled up his sleeves as though he meant business. The cats came running after him, following him everywhere. He opened his herb bag and spread the various plants out in the firelight. He seemed to find some difficulty in deciding which was the Merlin's Grass and he had to refer to his drawings and notes, and his glasses kept steaming up.

At last he seemed satisfied, for he nodded his tall black hat and smiled evilly to himself. Helda shut her eyes tight. She stood bolt upright, indeed, she could not do otherwise for it was as if she were turned to stone. Even though her eyes were shut she could see the dancing firelight through her closed lids.

Wizard Homm took two pieces of Merlin's Grass. He put them carefully in a small metal can with a wire handle, like those that tramps used to carry with them on their travels. Pouring in a little water, he put a long stick through the handle and suspended it over the fire.

The red flames were reflected on his tall black hat and a huge shadow was cast from him against the background of trees. Now for it!

Unless something very surprising happened it looked as though Helda would soon be turned into a donkey!

11

DRAGONS DON'T FORGET

HELDA couldn't resist opening her eyes for just one peep. The Wizard now had his back to her. The brew was boiling, she could hear it making a 'quaddling' noise in the tin. It would soon be all over with her now!

But what was this? Surely Ding, Dong, and Belle were behaving rather strangely! They were no longer watching the fire. All three were staring past it at the wall of green forest where the shadows made black canyons among the leaves. And Helda noticed their back fur was rising and their ears were flat.

Evidently the Wizard had not seen this. He was far too busy over his brew, muttering to himself and stirring busily. Against the fire the black hat looked exactly like a drainpipe, and the light, shining on either side of his head, made quite a saint-like halo of his whiskers, which was not at all suited to the subject.

Then – with a spitting noise, Ding, Dong, and Belle darted off sideways into the darkness.

This time the Wizard *did* notice something was amiss. He stopped stirring, he sat back on his heels. Those cats of his were good watchdogs, and they had taken fright at something. Whatever had alarmed them?

Helda held her breath. She sensed that something was about to happen, something very exciting. She thought she heard a faint snapping of branches from beyond the cave, where the yews grew thickly. There followed a faint brushing noise, as though something big was pushing through the thick underwood, something which was not making any effort to travel silently like all wild creatures in the Forest of Boland. Helda fancied, too, that she heard heavy breathing.

The Wizard had certainly heard it. He put down the can quickly, which was steaming in the firelight, and he gathered his blue gown about him. His limbs were trembling.

Nearer came the sounds, more distinct each moment. The Wizard was now very agitated. He looked about him, he turned and glowered suspiciously at Helda standing there within her circle, which now, incidentally, was hardly showing any glow at all on the grass. And then Wizard Homm did a *very* stupid thing. I can only suppose that the *Highland Dew* was to blame, or perhaps he remembered his bag of gold and thought someone had come to steal it.

He walked quickly across to the cave and vanished inside!

Helda moved her feet. It was strange, but they no longer felt heavy and immovable. The Wizard's spell was wearing off. She stepped over the circle. As she passed over it, it was exactly as if she had received a mild electric shock up her legs – only she could not have described it like that, of course. She gave a jump and a little gasp but she was outside the circle !

She ran across the clearing and hid behind one of the mossy blocks of stone from which grew the spreading yew. She felt she *must* see what was going to happen, for the noise in the Forest was very near now and the Wizard was evidently hiding in the cave, scared out of his wits, so there was no danger from him.

A moment later there emerged from the shadows the monstrous, mailed head of a dragon. The firelight played on its polished scales, it blazed in its big eyes fringed with heavy blonde lashes. Its slobbering nose was close to the ground. It seemed to be puzzling out a scent. Helda gave a shiver of fright – in fact, she was so frightened that she couldn't move a muscle, though she was now quite free from the Wizard's spell. But the dragon meant no harm to *her*, o dear no !

Quite slowly the vast creature emerged into the firelight, snuffling like a gigantic spaniel. After the long plated neck came the barrel body, then the long scaly tail. Once it stopped snuffling and glared mildly at the fire, in a puzzled way, then it began to grope its way slowly towards the cave, as a hunting dog smells out a game trail.

Just outside the cave was the Wizard's deck-chair. On the grass beside it was his massive book of magic and bag of herbs.

Fascinated, Helda saw the dragon's long pendulous lips groping about. First it ate the chair (the wood made a splintering noise as it scrunched it up). It gave a prodigious swallow. Next it picked up the book. It chewed that up, too, slowly and with relish, while saliva dribbled down out of the corners of its mouth. The bag of herbs, for some reason, it found not to its taste, and after looking thoughtful it spat this out again.

Next it found a small bottle lying in the grass, a bottle which was half-full of a *bright turquoise-blue liquid*! Slowly the truth dawned in that dim old brain! This bottle contained Dragon's Blood - its own blood - and it remembered what happened by the stream! For some moments it remained wrapped in thought - its brows wrinkling like those of a cow.

Helda, breathless, watched the great mailed creature, with the firelight winking on its scales as though on armour. Then it turned about and with ponderous tread advanced towards the cave. Helda, no longer scared, could have clapped her hands with delight, for she imagined the Wizard crouching terrified in the inmost recesses. The dragon moved with the leisurely dignified tread of an elephant, dragging its scaly tail behind it, its fat scaly legs somewhat bowed.

Helda stared at the dark cavern where the ivy creepers hung down, each pointed leaf shining like metal in the dying firelight. Then the entrance was filled entirely by the dragon as it slowly passed

inside. First its head entered, then the huge barrel body, and finally the long scaly tail, which was slowly sucked from sight like a monstrous worm disappearing down its burrow.

All was now silent. The fire, no longer flaming, was a mass of red embers. The Wizard's tin, outlined blackly against the glow, suddenly fell on its side as a charred stick gave way and there was a sharp hissing sound as the liquid met the hot embers.

When the Wizard ran into the cave, I'm afraid he had quite lost his head. If he had stopped to think, as a wise Wizard should have done, he might at least have taken his book of spells with him. When he remembered that, it was too late. It might have been possible, even then, for him to have disappeared, for it was a spell he had practised many times. But his bag of herbs was outside too, and, anyway, you can't make magic all in a moment.

There was no light inside the cave. The Wizard, in his hurry, kept falling over various objects. He finished up by tripping headlong over his bag of gold. He barked his shin and it was so painful he began to curse loudly, hopping round on one leg, which, again, was a *most* stupid thing to do, for the dragon heard him quite clearly.

Wizard Homm squeezed himself up in one corner – it wasn't a large cave – and waited, hoping for the best. Whatever the creature was, perhaps it would soon go away. If it was a wild boar, or a bear, it would certainly take fright at the fire. When it had left he would go back and finish the spell of turning Helda into a donkey. It was really *most* annoying, being disturbed like this in the middle of such an important spell, the best he'd ever tried.

Just then the dim arch of light in the cave mouth darkened. The dragon's head looked in.

What followed, I will leave to your imagination. In fact, I do not think I will describe the next few minutes in detail.

The dragon, who could see very well in the dark, recognized at once the black stove-pipe hat, for dragons, like elephants, never forget. The last time the dragon had seen that hat, it was poking above the sallow bushes on the banks of the stream, the day the stone had rolled down and hit it on the nose. And it just put two and two together.

Normally, this particular dragon ate herbs and would never have dreamt of eating anyone, but now a little meat would make a change of diet. Somehow, just then, the dragon felt in need of it, and there was an old score to pay.

So if you must know the brutal truth, the dragon ate Wizard Homm, quite leisurely, stove-pipe hat, blue gown, and all!

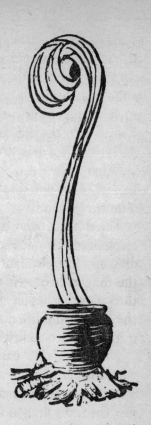

12

CONCLUSION

As you may have guessed, we are now at the end of my story. You know what happened to the Wizard. What of the goose-girl, and what became of the dragon? And we mustn't forget the Wizard's cats!

Well, the dragon found this new cave so much more to its liking that it decided to settle down there. For one thing, it was a much smaller, more compact cave than his old one at Poolewe, and *much* more snug and quiet, and he wasn't bothered with gnomes going in and out and making a racket with their picks and shovels and their puffing train.

It is quite true that for a few days after he had eaten the Wizard he suffered from a tummy-upset. But the trouble soon settled down and the poor old thing was able to tuck himself up again and go to sleep. Indeed, he's probably there now at this very moment, snoring away to his heart's content and not troubled by anyone! I don't think that even the gnomes know he is there, for the cave is off the beaten track and some way from his old home.

Of course, the Wizard's bag of ill-gotten gold must still be there too, but as the dragon is using it as a pillow I doubt if anyone will care to remove it. I certainly would not like to do so.

What of little Helda? That is almost another book in itself. I think things might well have gone badly with her if the cowzies hadn't found her again and obligingly showed her the way out of the Forest of Boland. It was a long march. By the time she got home she was very footsore. She found her family safe and well and the village rebuilt, and there were no more floods.

Ding, Dong, and Belle, had been so scared by the dragon that they ran for several miles without stopping. Then they decided that they wouldn't go back to the Wizard, which was perhaps a wise decision. If they had, the dragon would certainly have eaten them up. No matter, cats are always able to

look after themselves. In point of fact, all three kittens married and had families. They met up with some wild cats in the Forest of Boland, which accounted for the black and white wild ones which were occasionally seen by the gnomes for many years afterwards.

With the Wizard, and the dragon, and Helda well out of the way, the gnomes soon settled down again to their normal way of life. They repaired the railway, they mended the bridges, and though, at times, Hal o' the Hobb wondered where the old dragon had got to, he didn't worry overmuch and kept his fears to himself.

In later years little Helda married and had a large family of brown children. Sometimes as she sat playing with them on summer evenings down by the stream, where the white geese trooped to drink, and the slow oxen grazed, she looked across the valley to the huge mass of the trees and wondered what her friends the cowzies were doing, whether the dragon was still in the Wizard's cave, and whether the little gnome she had seen was still mounting guard by the bridge over the stream.

And she would watch, by the hour, the steady, crinkled current of the Boland Water, hurrying on its way towards the dark Forest, and she would listen to the murmur of its ripples over the stones.

Only the Boland Water knew the answers to her questions. But the language of the bright streams is not for human understanding. Next time you hear a stream talking to itself you will hear, if you listen long enough, low musical voices which are certainly saying something in a language all their own, but, like Helda, you will never understand what they are trying to tell you. Only the Little People in the dark Forest can understand, which is perhaps just as well.

THE FOREST OF BOLAND LIGHT RAILWAY

'BB'

One of the most famous and popular of modern fantasies, now in paperback for the first time as a result of public demand

The Forest of Boland Light Railway, with its magnificent steam engine the *Boland Belle*, is the pride and joy of the gnomes who live in the Forest. But one day their enemies the leprechauns overcome the gnomes in a surprise attack, and drag them off to their stronghold, Castle Shera. The outlook seems bleak, but the cowzies come to the rescue just in time.

These are other Knight Books

NURSE MATILDA

Christianna Brand

Mr and Mrs Brown were always having great difficulty with their numerous and incredibly naughty children. They tried all the agencies but nurses, governesses and nannies never stayed long with the Brown children. 'The person *you* want is Nurse Matilda,' they were told. And when Nurse Matilda does arrive, strange things begin to happen.

NURSE MATILDA GOES TO TOWN

Christianna Brand

Once Nurse Matilda made Mr and Mrs Brown's huge family of incredibly naughty children all good and well-behaved, but now they are naughty again. The children go to stay with Great-Aunt Adelaide in London – and once more Nurse Matilda has to be called to the rescue.

THE ROBBER HOTZENPLOTZ
Otfried Preussler

The wicked robber Hotzenplotz was
the terror of the village. Whatever he
wanted he stole and he was always armed
with a sword, a pistol and seven knives.
Then he took Grandmother's musical
coffee mill and Kasperl and Seppel just
had to do something about it. But the
ingenious plan misfired and robber
Hotzenplotz captured them both. When
Kasperl was sold to the great magician
Petrosilius Zackleman there seemed no
no way of disentangling themselves from
such a fix.

THE FURTHER ADVENTURES
OF THE ROBBER HOTZENPLOTZ
Otfried Preussler

The robber Hotzenplotz escaped from
prison, still as wicked as ever. And
something just had to be done about it, so
off went Kasperl and Seppel to trap him.
Then everything went sadly wrong and he
kidnapped Grandmother and captured
them both too. All seemed lost until a
crocodile-dog called Fido arrived on the
scene and justice triumphed once again.

THE LITTLE BROOMSTICK
Mary Stewart

Nothing could ever happen here, thought
Mary, exiled to Great-Aunt Charlotte's
house. But she was wrong. That very
day Tib the cat led her to a curious
flower called fly-by-night. Then she
found a little broomstick hidden in a
corner – and her strange and wonderful
magic adventure had begun.

Ask your local bookseller, or at your
public library, for details of other Knight
Books, or write to the Editor-in-Chief,
Knight Books, Arlen House, Salisbury
Road, Leicester LE1 7QS